THE GREEK TEACHER

By

MICHAEL JAMES GOULD

The year is 1965. Down from Oxford, Percy Spenser starts teaching in a suburban boys' grammar school.

The characters and events described in this novel are wholly fictitious, and any similarity to persons living or dead or events that took place is purely coincidental.

michaelgould7@hotmail.com

ISBN

978–1–0686112–0–9

Michael James Gould

Chapters

Chapter One

Staff Meeting Monday 6th September 1965

It wasn't exactly love at first sight. It couldn't have been. Elvira Thompson was, after all, forty years older than Percy Spenser; but down from Brasenose with a double first, he was exactly right for the post of a junior master to teach Latin and Greek at Hurstwood Grammar School for boys, the appointee having given last minute notice. He had short, curly blond hair and a pinkish complexion, with slight beads of sweat glistening on his forehead. It was a hot day to be so immaculately clad in a Prince of Wales check suit, with long-sleeved shirt and maroon tie. She was far more comfortably attired in a well-worn plain grey summer dress. She had a wizened face, without the slightest hint of make-up, and iron-grey hair cut in a school girl style. They smiled warmly at each other. He was the only applicant, she the sole interviewer, the headmaster being away on important business involving an alcoholic lunch, Mr Tourtel, her most senior assistant, on holiday in Italy, investigating the Appian Way, and Mr Rowntree, the more junior assistant, who was earmarked to succeed to the departmental headship on her retirement, not having been asked.

The briefing she gave him was perhaps not as comprehensive as it might have been. Matters were in the lap of the gods and the headmaster, Captain Turpin, known by the boys as Dirty Dick, although she didn't allude to his nickname. There were always last-minute surprises at the staff meeting. He would of course attend on Monday 6th September 1965. He assured her most certainly that he would, and the date itself went down in his memory as the start of a whole new life.

He crept into the staffroom cautiously that morning, though slightly later than intended, and espied Mrs Thompson pouring out cups of tea. "I'd take the seat by the open window," she said, handing him a cup of dark brown liquid. Percy duly took her advice. The air was already blue

1

with smoke. Outside he could see a grey-haired man almost sprinting across the rugby pitch. As he drew closer, Percy could see the man's sun-tanned face, shabby blazer, and white cotton trousers of the type his mother bought his father from Marks and Spencer.

The staff meeting was scheduled to start promptly with the head's arrival at nine o'clock. The question was whether the puffing gentleman would make the staffroom before the headmaster or not. To cheer him on would not have been entirely proper, though Percy sensed he wasn't the only one watching the spectacle. The gentleman succeeded, however, sat next to Percy, and promptly opened a fresh pack of Players cigarettes. "I can't bear those tipped things my wife smokes," he said, offering Percy one. "My name's Vincent Tourtel, by the way, Latin, English and Greek, if they'll let me."

Percy apologised for the social crime of not smoking, despite the discomfort he was forced to endure on a regular basis, and imparted that he was Percy Spenser, to teach Latin and Greek. He inferred there might be important staff room politics, and was anxious not to have stolen any of Mr Tourtel's timetable, but Mr Tourtel had now enquired where he was down from, and was delighted to hear they were both BNC men.

At that moment the headmaster flung the door open, and whilst the sitting teachers stood up metaphorically, those who were standing froze to attention. All thought he'd put on even more weight over the holidays—doubtless, the more weight to throw about!

"A cup of tea, headmaster?" said Mrs Thompson, who could be relied on to put down the mighty from their seat, without their noticing it.

"You are too kind, Mrs Thompson," he replied, and was about to add, "My kingdom is not of this world," his mind being on a sermon he was writing in his capacity as a Methodist lay preacher, but thought better of the remark. "I'm full to the gills. Shall we start."

He realised at that point that no order paper had been distributed. What were the secretaries up to? Recalling, however, Mrs Rothwell's muffled complaints about the Gestetner, he swept in with apologies, and invited staff to remind him in due course of anything he might have missed.

"First, you may have heard whispers about the appointment of a young lady to teach maths. The said young lady, Miss Allsop, is unable to attend today, alas. I'm sure, when you get to meet her, you will realise just how accomplished she is, and what a credit to the school she will doubtless be; but I did feel on meeting her that her style of dress and make-up could be described as overly glamorous. Frankly, boys can get excited enough without the fragrance of Chanel number five, and I hope she might dress with more decorum. Mrs Thompson, you have always set a good example in this respect, and I think you might have words with her."

He was about to add, perhaps you could introduce her to your tailor, but didn't; and she was about to say, "O woe is me, for I am undone," a line which came into her head without being readily relevant.

"I don't want Miss Allsop," he continued, "to be embarrassed by any form of crudeness. I particularly remind the biology staff not to leave on any blackboard the representation of a cross-section of human sexual intercourse. Sex education should not get out of hand. Now, I had an anonymous letter of complaint from someone purporting to be the father of one of the junior boys, alleging he, the boy that is, was followed into the junior lavatories by a certain master. Analysis of the handwriting against the signature of parent or guardian attesting to their reading of school reports has not been conclusive. I am, therefore, unable to name the boy making this vicious libel. I do remind staff that ordinary supervision is open to misinterpretation, even if I very much doubt any of our masters, and certainly not the master named, would have impure motives."

3

The staff were most intrigued by this revelation, but it was the headmaster's habit to throw in an item of human interest before they switched off. He knew they were solely interested in their timetable for the year, but he was only going to get round to that by way of compulsory contributions to the Pestalozzi Children's Village (forms in each year were obliged to compete with regard to donations for his chosen charity); a list of the scheduled events for the term, including parent evenings, the carol concert and the informal concert; expansion of the number of prefects to ensure a crack-down on boys smoking on the bus; after-school activities, clubs and societies etc. Once he was on to timetable subjects, the teachers would withdraw for a detailed conference with the subject head, and a further trip to operation headquarters where the timetable was being fine-tuned by the head of the maths department, traditionally deemed the most suitable person to work it all out and receive the flak.

English and Latin were usually last on the list, but for no good reason. Percy had been concentrating like mad, listening to every detail relevant to physics, chemistry, maths etc, but noticed Mr Tourtel starting to nod off, when the head dropped a bombshell.

"And now we come to English. You may well have noticed that Mr McKenzie is not here. You may have heard he has left us. I had words with him last term for the inordinate length of his last theatrical production, Marlowe's *Dr Faustus*, when those too foolish to leave at the interval or walk out during the second half, missed their last bus. Fortunately, everybody got home safely, as far as we know, but we were inundated with complaints. I informed Mr McKenzie he could not direct Marlowe's *Edward II* as he was planning this year. It is a most unsuitable play, even if it is on the A-level syllabus. Mr McKenzie has since found another teaching post at short notice. I have decided therefore Mr Tourtel will replace him. But as Mr Tourtel will need to teach some Latin classes, but not Greek, we will still be short of the required staffing for the English department at former levels. The best economy is to combine the two sixth-form English sets. It has been an unnecessary luxury having two classes of fifteen instead of one class of thirty. The rationale, I believe, was to encourage boys to contribute to discussion, but from my experience no one ever says anything anyway."

Mr Tourtel followed the English staff out of the meeting room, and was thus unable to find out the new classics master plan.

"My intentions for classics teaching and its contribution to our Oxford and Cambridge intake," the head addressed the remaining three members. "Mr Spenser, meet Mrs Thompson and Mr Rowntree." The three nodded to each other, realising this was not yet their cue for social intercourse. "I have decided ancient history A-level is to be added to the timetable. All boys studying Latin and Greek will study ancient history. They may study this in place of their normal third A-level, or in addition to it, but it will be mandatory. Mr Rowntree, you will teach Roman history, with which I am sure you are familiar, and Mr Spenser, you will teach Greek. I regret the shortage of time for preparing the course. I believe Mrs Thompson has obtained details of the syllabus and former exam papers. That will be all, unless there are any questions."

The headmaster said this, rising from his chair to signify he didn't want to answer any questions anyway, and therefore it wasn't unreasonable not to allow anyone time to think of any; and Mrs Thompson took over the chair. She remained smitten with Mr Spenser, admiring his academic prowess and intellect with his Oxford degree, but feared that he might have discipline problems. Mr Rowntree was unable to see Mr Spenser as a threat to his obtaining the post of department head, and therefore saw him as a most useful work horse. Mr Rowntree, whose forenames Jocelyn Alexis had given rise to the appellations Josh, Smart Alec and Smarticus, following the film Spartacus, may have had intelligence, but was not instinctively interested in the Latin language, Latin literature, Roman history, or classical culture. He admired the

5

discipline of the Roman army with its infliction of an arduous regime on the fighting troops. Unable to be a commanding officer in an army of long ago, he contented himself with drilling junior pupils in conjugations and declensions, and interrogating them in a terrifying manner. It was a moot point whether Mrs Thompson was aware of this or not. He always showed her the greatest respect. Mrs Thompson had her doubts whether with reduced assistance from Mr Tourtel, they could cover all their periods. It was likely the periods allocated to teaching O-level Latin in the sixth form would need to be curtailed. There was much to discuss before going to the operations room.

Mr Tourtel, however displeased at the probable loss of the head of department post, and the teaching of Cicero's *Pro Milone* to the upper sixth Latin class, after his researches into the geography of the Appian Way, where Milo had killed Clodius, was highly gratified to be given the combined upper sixth-modern English class. Although he hadn't read the set books in the summer holidays, as he would otherwise have done, they were all books he had read before, apart from Virginia Woolf's *To the Lighthouse*. With Chaucer's *Prologue to the Canterbury Tales* and T. S. Eliot's *Murder in the Cathedral* being on the syllabus, he thought a trip to Canterbury Cathedral was essential, and might well be fun; but he didn't envisage staging *the Winter's Tale* or *Antony and Cleopatra*. Mr McKenzie's departure gave him a free hand, and he thought he would direct *Julius Caesar* for the school's next production, which was on the O-level syllabus.

Meeting back in the staffroom, Mr Tourtel, living but a hundred yards from the school, invited Percy for lunch, and Percy was pleased to accept. The invitation was extended to Mrs Thompson and Mr Rowntree, but they were anxious to return to their respective spouses, and perhaps rather wary of what exactly was on offer.

The Tourtels' house was in the chalet style favoured by some interwar builders, and common throughout London suburbia. The third bedroom and bathroom were downstairs, convenient no doubt for sick children needing nursing and arthritic grandmothers, whilst the front door was at the side. Mr Tourtel explained that rather than a howling draught blowing through the house, it simply blew upstairs, where the two double bedrooms opened out perilously onto a tiny landing.

The Tourtels had only returned from Italy the day before, and all was untidiness and mess, quite anathema to Percy. Moreover, Mrs Tourtel had clearly been shopping that morning, and the groceries were no more unpacked and put away than their luggage. Mrs Tourtel was quite unfazed by the guest her husband ought not to have invited. She had a handy knack for befriending and interrogating all such. His entire life story was there to be revealed over lunch, if there were to be any.

"Go and get some fish and chips," she said, dispatching her husband forcefully into the nearby town, "and if the shop's not open, buy something from the baker's." He looked dutifully obedient in an almost pathetic way, as he grabbed an ancient shopping bag, not quite downgraded to use only for potatoes, and beat a hasty retreat.

Steering Percy through the dining room and into the adjacent kitchen, she ordered him to tell her all about himself, and began chopping up a lettuce in a very casual manner.

"You wouldn't guess from my speech that I come from Truro," he said, rising to the occasion by affecting a rather pompous style, "but all traces of a Cornish accent were beaten out of me at the King's School Canterbury, to which charitable institution my father sent my twin brother and me at vast expense. He was a doctor, who claimed to have been ruined by the NHS. I fear he blew his inheritance on our education, especially the tennis lessons, which were extra, and quite considerably so."

"You play tennis," exclaimed Mrs Tourtel with excitement. "So do Vincent and I at the local club. You must join."

7

Percy was a little defensive. "Well, you see, William, my twin, and I got to be quite good, embarrassingly good for ordinary club play, but never quite up to professional standards. I was recently encouraged to take up golf."

"Take up golf, by all means," said Mrs Tourtel, "but tennis clubs in general, and ours in particular, are always looking for near professionals to give lessons and coach. We have a junior section and desperately need an instructor. You can give some of the older members lessons too, particularly where to stand when playing doubles. You can start this Saturday."

Mrs Tourtel was prevented from making further appropriations of Percy's timetable by the prompt arrival of her husband with pasties and pies from the local baker's shop. It was debatable whether he had even attempted the possibly fruitless journey to the fish and chip shop. By this time, she had heated a couple of cans of unbranded vegetable soup. Flinging open the French windows of the dining room, she was about to suggest alfresco, but the patio table had suffered the ravages of pigeons and starlings throughout the summer. They stayed indoors, but appreciated the breeze.

"So, what is your abiding impression of Brasenose?" asked Mr Tourtel, careful to alternate between BNC and Brasenose, but never to say Brasenose College, which would have amounted to a sin against the Holy Ghost.

"The shortage of bath tubs," said Percy with surprising animation. "It was astonishingly difficult to keep clean. It was even worse when I lived in Jericho. There was a tiny kitchen sink and an outdoor toilet. I had a beautiful matching china bowl and jug with which to perform ablutions in my bedroom. The water didn't quite freeze over on a frosty night. There was a choice between the public baths and a long queue for the BNC tubs."

The Tourtels were highly amused.

"Was there any particular reason for coming to Hurstwood?" Mr Tourtel asked.

"Mandy Russell," he replied, parting with his secret sorrows in a somewhat forthright manner. "She was my girl-friend at Oxford. She's been teaching at the Church of England School on the corner for the last year."

Mrs Tourtel's face lit up. "That's where I teach. I know her."

"Mandy was at the Lady Spencer Churchill Teacher Training College, and resident in Jericho when I was there. Not quite. She had friends in Jericho, but was living over a butcher's shop in Little Clarendon Street. Her college drama group used to put on plays in the Oxford Playhouse, inviting Oxford University students to join them. In my second year, her final year, I played Pierre Cauchon in Jean Anouilh's *The Lark*, while she played Joan. The romance has really sort of fizzled out. I'm trying to renew my suit, but I'm getting on better with her mother, who wants me to join their golf club, the Beech Estate."

"That would upset Josh," said Mr Tourtel with the ghost of a smile on his face. "That's Mr Rowntree. He's been trying to join local golf clubs, but without success."

"Where are you living?" said Mrs Tourtel, changing the subject.

"I'm afraid I have the most awful digs. They are quite close, though. One bath a week, and compulsory breakfast and dinner

"Sounds like BNC," said Mr Tourtel. "You might ask Mr Townsend if he has accommodation. He's history. Instantly recognisable, rotund and bald. But he lives some way out. You'd need a car, if not to be dependent on the Greenline coach and a bus."

Percy knew instantly who Mr Tourtel meant. He had noticed a very fat man, whose underpants appeared to be attached by loops to buttons inside his trouser band, whilst ancient leather braces attached to other buttons in the band held up the trousers. The fact that his shirt was therefore tucked inside his underpants seemed slightly indecent to Percy. The spectacle had brought to mind his landlord in Jericho, retired P.C. Parsons, who was wont to shave at the kitchen sink, the braces of his trousers hanging down at the side.

"Let me invite you and Mandy to tea. That might help a reconciliation," suggested Mrs Tourtel, though she knew well that Miss Russel appeared sweet on Mark Thornby, a teacher who had joined the school in the summer term, a bearded weirdo, in Mrs Tourtel's opinion, especially as he resisted all her attempts at interrogation.

"You know she has a younger brother at the school. He's likely to be in your Greek class."

"Yes, I do," said Percy.

Percy didn't leave until he had signed up to conduct tennis coaching, and attend for afternoon tea at the earliest opportunity, when Mandy would be invited. He was also permitted a brief gaze at Mr Tourtel's fine book collection of classical texts and commentaries, and encouraged to show interest in viewing Mr Tourtel's colour slides of Italy at an unspecified future date.

Chapter Two

First Day of Term Wednesday 8th September 1965

The Home Service was on in the background on the landlady's 1940s Ferguson, as Percy manfully attacked her cooked English breakfast. He could hardly listen to the news for worry about his classes, timetable and everything else. He didn't even know his way round the school, no one having thought fit to show him. He was to be the form master of a junior form, with responsibility for keeping the register and appointment of class monitors. He had had no briefing about this, nor about sick notes, dinner money, the sports fund, the school magazine, and the school rules, particularly the dress code. He had an idea that school blazers were meant to be worn at all times, however hot the day, and it promised to be a scorcher, though permission might be given for their removal during class. He was, of course, as much a victim of these rules himself, being expected to wear his academic gown over suit or sports jacket, and under no circumstances to remove his tie. It could be worse, he mused, had he been a barrister, and added wig and waistcoat to the mountain of unnecessary clothing. His father's idea of enjoyment was simply to wear shorts and a tee-shirt on a hot day, even if he got a little sunburnt.

His provisional timetable was four Latin classes, dispersed through the five years of the junior school, and the fifth-year Greek class, amounting to twenty-five periods; and eight periods of Greek in the lower sixth, two for unseen translation, two for prose composition, two for set books and two for ancient history. That totalled thirty-three. He had also volunteered to take his form for R.I., which took it to thirty-four, leaving but one free period.

But as had been pointed out to him, the junior school work involved him in very little marking outside the classroom, there being no essays, whilst all homework could be marked in class. The text books seemed

11

remarkably old-fashioned. *The Clarendon Latin Course* seemed to belong in a museum, but clearly Mrs Thompson swore by it. Mr Rowntree swore by keeping the junior school on their feet, whilst selected individuals delivered principal parts of verbs with a ruler pointed in their face.

The morning seemed to pass quite smoothly, and at lunch/dinner he found himself sitting opposite the new maths mistress, animadverted to by the headmaster at the staff meeting. He was quite smitten, but found himself discussing his whole affair with Mandy, without quite mentioning her brother was at the school. She was a sympathetic listener, but revealed little about herself, except that she rented a room in a rooming house, the other tenants were women, there was a payphone on the landing, and a common kitchen and bathroom with a hungry gas meter.

Back in the staffroom Mr Morgan Townsend introduced himself, with the explanation that he was head of the history department designate, and actual head of the R.I. department, though R.I. was not taught to O-level. This surprised Percy. It was known to be easy, and it could be done with a portion of the New Testament in Greek.

"Happen," Mr Townsend remarked, affecting a Yorkshire accent, "But not here. Head has other ideas, though he be a Methodist lay preacher. I claim the allowance for being head of the department, but do little beyond choosing the readings for assembly."

"Don't you use the Church of England lectionary?" Percy asked timorously.

"Good heavens, no. I decide the following week's lessons on a Friday afternoon."

"But how does the reader discover them?"

"The vice-head boy puts the prefects on a rota, and woe betide them if they don't see me at 4 pm sharp on the Friday. Now, first year R.I. is as follows: term one Genesis, term two Exodus, and term three Mark. Teach it any way you like. The boys are all expected to bring their own Authorised Version, but personally I use the Revised. The Revised Standard Version and Moffatt are complete anathema, by the way, and especially that J.B. Philips the Christian Union are so fond of. I don't want any of that."

That afternoon he had his first period with his sixth form Greek class. Tim studiously gave no indication that he knew Percy, and avoided his gaze, though this seemed to remind him of one of the poses the boy's sister adopted in pretending she wasn't talking to him. He handed out Bury's *History of Greece to the Death of Alexander the Great*, explaining he couldn't hope to be much more than a chapter ahead of them, detailed history having been hardly supported by a degree course involving reading the entire *Iliad* in Greek, prodigious amounts of Herodotus and Plato, and at least half of the extant forty-four Greek tragedies and comedies. Let the dead Bury their dead, as Tim said looking up and laughing.

"Indeed," said Percy, and commenced an unseen translation, entirely unseen by himself. Translation came very easily to him, but more importantly he had a good knack for explaining the inherent problems of grammar, syntax and meaning.

Chapter Three

Tea at the Tourtels

Percy had signed up for what was variously known as school dinner or school lunch, though he would have preferred sandwiches. The latter option was difficult. His landlady was unlikely to make anything acceptable to a man from BNC, but would never have let him into the kitchen to make his own. Even if she did, the dog wouldn't. There were two rather insalubrious cafes in Hurstwood High Street, always busy, the fish and chip bar by the station, which always appeared to be shut, and the nice baker's shop where Mr Tourtel had bought the meat pies. The nice baker's shop didn't open till nine, and had long queues in perpetuity, the woman behind the counter being painfully slow. The annexe to the school canteen was thus the default option, where the staff were accommodated in grander fashion than the boys. Pursuant to a design thought up by the art master, there was an unfinished mural on the rear wall a pupil with more enthusiasm than talent was attempting to paint. The headmaster was framed by the Three Graces, and all eyes were drawn to Michelangelo's David, against the better instincts of their owners. There were two sittings, and the regulars always sat in the same places. In consequence he found himself regularly sitting with Chris Allsop, which was delightful, and helped take his mind off his broken heart.

The Friday of that first week he was invited to tea at the Tourtels to which Mandy had also been invited. After his landlady's breakfast, the school dinner, and with his landlady's tea to follow at six thirty, Percy was hardly anxious to consume slices of fruit cake, scones, apple pie, sandwiches and sponge cake, let alone jellies or trifle, but everything was available. The sideboard was piled high, and on the centre of the round table was a turntable which enabled you to move the desired item into the right position for your plate. Percy had not noticed the swivel top on his earlier visit. Mandy, who had always had a good appetite and

14

had a sweet tooth, was in her seventh heaven. She rarely ate such items at home on account of her father's diabetes. Mrs Tourtel explained that she liked baking, but disliked vegetable preparation, something which might have been inferred from her treatment of the luckless lettuce on Monday. During term times they ate school dinners, and went without a cooked meal in the evening. Mandy was pleased to see Percy again, and he to see her. She enthused about the job and the opportunities for drama with the pupils. She mentioned a male teacher who also had good ideas and worked with her and Mrs Tourtel.

The meal was about to finish when a loud crash at the door indicated that Jospehine, the Tourtels' daughter, was back from the Art College. She looked in to say hallo rather blearily before wafting off to the summer house in the back garden. She was very striking with natural jet-black hair, and wore clothes which defied fashion or taste.

"Can I see you home, Mandy?" Percy asked, careless of the potential snub to his landlady, who would be expecting him back for something quite unappetising or badly cooked, and described as "tea."

"I've got lessons to prepare, and I'm sure you have. How about a matinee in town Saturday or a show somewhere? Think of something."

He walked her to the bus stop, thinking he should get himself a car. They hadn't mentioned her brother.

When he got back to his lodgings, with little enthusiasm for Mrs Smedley's cooked tea, he was surprised to find a letter addressed to him in a familiar hand. It was from Jeremy Wright, or Jet as he was always known, from his frequent jet streams round the streets of Oxford in the course of sampling the city's famous ales.

Hello, old thing. I've tracked you down at last. Sorry about my financial crisis and all that! What a bore, what a bore, but now I'm making a mint in the city. All the right connections, old school tie, you know.

15

Here's a cheque for some of what I owe. Cash it quick before it bounces. As you can see from the address, I've got a squalid dive off the King's Road, Chelsea. Come up for drinks. Bring a friend. Jet—Phone number FLA 2312

In his first year, Percy had got involved with Jet, initially because both were amateur botanists; but Jet modelled himself on Sebastian Flyte in *Brideshead Revisited*, and had gathered together a little set of camp followers, which Percy soon joined. A good time was had by all, but Jet had borrowed money from Percy which was supposed to be repaid out of a trust fund. Whether the trust fund existed or not, or had been spent several times over, was not clear, but Percy shouldn't have lent the money, and was left seriously out of pocket when Jet was sent down in disgrace. Percy recovered only a small amount from Jet's father, the Right Reverend Julian Wright. The cheque was for just enough to buy the Morris Minor the woman next door was selling after her husband's stroke. It was a low mileage car that had been well maintained. Percy was too soft-hearted to beat her down too much on the price. It was a bargain in any event. There was further correspondence from various insurance companies, anxious to sign him up for ten-year policies. Perhaps his new friend in the city could give advice. Jet had been studying maths, after all, and had quite a sharp brain, when he chose to apply it; but that wasn't very often.

Chapter Four

Eventful Saturdays

It was obvious that it was over with Mandy. Mrs Russell had spoken to him over the phone, and lamented Mandy's new boyfriend, who had no business to be teaching at a Church of England school when he had a beard. Mrs Russell detested beards. She was quite enamoured of Percy, and would keep him on the phone much longer than desirable, but she said she might get him into the golf club. It seemed a strange consolation for the loss of one he still loved. Mrs Tourtel had now arranged for him to do a coaching session with the juniors at her tennis club on Saturday mornings.

That first Saturday the coaching went extremely well. The juniors were in their teens, so after a formal lesson, he organised some doubles play. After two hours, the club secretary said they wanted the courts for the adults, but invited him to join in their social play. He soon upset one of the senior ladies by suggesting she played nearer the net. "I know where the ball's going. No one tells me where to stand." Mrs Tourtel told him not to take any notice. "She's a difficult woman." It was everything Percy disliked about tennis clubs. There were always difficult women who wouldn't be told. He availed himself of the club's cold shower.

Mrs Tourtel was most insistent Percy should accompany her after tennis to the hunger lunch in the church hall. The vicar was most concerned about third world nutrition, banning the bomb and protesting about the war in Vietnam. He wasn't much interested in missionary work or the finer points of Christian doctrine. Of course, there was a faction in the congregation that opposed him, thinking him a communist and an atheist. He should be preaching gospel sermons and challenging the congregation with the question, "What must I do to be saved?"

"What should they do, then?" Percy asked Mrs Tourtel, fascinated by her account of the ongoing debate in All Saints, Hurstwood. "Sign a petition, of course," she replied, "or rattle a tambourine." Percy didn't think he could include this observation in his R.I. class, but did wonder which Greek god had introduced the tambourine, probably Dionysus, along with the flute and drum

Percy's idea of a hunger lunch was going without any. He was surprised by the generous slab of cheese to go with the French bread from the nice baker's with the long queue, and parted with a full four shillings. The celery was good too, thoughtfully provided by the organisers. He duly signed the petition and discussed Greek with the vicar, who confessed he'd forgotten what he learned at theological college. He was a Cambridge man with a degree in maths, and owned to having received the call, after failing to solve Hilbert's Thirteenth Problem. Neither Percy nor Mrs Tourtel could understand the nature of the problem which had been solved by Kolmogorov in 1957, and the vicar confessed he no longer understood it himself. Maths' loss was the church's gain, or not, depending which pew you sat in.

The following Saturday Jet had promised to get tickets to see the uncensored version of *A Patriot for Me* by John Osborne, showing at the Royal Court Theatre Club. Jet had explained the artificial way a supposed private theatre club had been set up to bypass the Lord Chamberlain's censorship, but it was entirely under the control of the theatre management, and members never actually got to attend Annual General Meetings or elect a committee. However, the members' club pretence involved being proposed by the person in the box office and seconded by someone else. This involved a ten-day wait for your membership card, before you could book a show. The upshot was they couldn't get tickets. Percy had originally hoped just to take Mandy to the show; but now it seemed, entirely against his better judgement, he was taking Mandy, her new boyfriend, the bearded teacher, and Tim, who wasn't old enough to drink, but would pass for eighteen, to meet Jet, have a few drinks and probably spend the night in Flood Street, where Jet had secured some lodgings, his residential landlord being away. Importantly, there was somewhere to park. Percy wished he was going on his own. The whole expedition seemed entirely doomed. Mrs Russell suggested she gave them all an early dinner, and would have given them some sandwiches to take as well for after the pub, if Mandy hadn't stopped her. Percy squirmed and felt uncomfortable in the presence of the new boyfriend, Mark Thornby, and his pupil. He could feel Mrs Russell's animosity to Mark.

He hadn't driven into London before, and on consulting the A to Z the obvious route seemed to be to cross Chelsea Bridge. He was cautioned against the South Circular, however, and ended up going via London Bridge and the Embankment. Somehow, they got to Flood Street and found the parking space. Jet was on form and soon had them ensconced in the Colville. It was a gay pub, and would be very packed later, but was just right for an early drink. They sat round a table, and Jet was soon rather drunk, but talking with great gusto about his role as a financial consultant. To be honest, he was really selling life insurance. The three young teachers had all been pestered to buy life insurance policies from every direction, and were interested in any genuine advice. Jet was very scathing about the standard 10- or 15-year policies heavily promoted to school and college leavers. Substantial commissions were paid to men like him for selling them. Their chief advantage was the tax relief on two fifths of the premiums. The companies, whether mutual or not, needed to invest their funds to best advantage, but had no satisfactory way to apportion the share between policy holders; and if you cashed in early, you might get little or nothing back. Could you really wait ten years? Should you go for the company which paid the highest bonuses at the expense of its reserves or a company with a modest pay out whose reserves seemed to increase exponentially? He deplored investment in government funds or gilts on the grounds that the interest was less than the amount by which the funds lost value due to inflation. He was scathing about the commercial property market, which was always about to go bust. Ordinary shares were the best investment, usually known as equities. "Here is some free advice, buy unit trusts which invest in equities in a savings plan that gets you the tax relief. The first two months' payments buy the life insurance. Thereafter you pay the 5% spread between the buying and selling price of the units, and the fund managers cream off 1% a year in a further charge. In the long run the units go up about 10% a year. At any time you can cash in, but might have to refund some of the tax relief within seven years. But when units go down in value your monthly payment buys more, and those units stand to increase substantially. Your time scale is three to five years for early profit. Save and Prosper are the market leader, then there's M & G. The commission works differently for chaps like me. But what you really want are good share tips. I've had a bit of luck I don't mind telling you. What is everybody having?"

On collecting the orders, Jet swept up to the bar. He certainly got admiring glances from those in the pub, some young and trendy, others rather old and seedy. He was wearing a green velvet suit and patterned shirt purchased from I Was Lord Kitchener's Valet. Tim thought Jet was too talented to be selling pension plans. Mandy thought he should be on the stage. Mark thought he should be in the fashion industry. Percy didn't know what to think, other than that Jet should find himself a rich lover to keep him in drink. Jet hadn't quite accounted for the basement flat he was lodging in. Perhaps he already had.

They ended the evening in a rather nice pub called the Fox and Hounds, before adjourning to Flood Street with some fish and chips. Jet mixed some cocktails, and their heads were soon spinning. Having organised some primitive sleeping arrangements, Jet said he was going off to the Gigolo, a nearby coffee bar of ill repute, and left them. He woke them all up coming back about three-thirty, having perhaps found somewhere to consume further alcohol.

Percy woke with a serious hangover a bit before nine. He lay there for a while, in acute discomfort, concluding that no one else would wake for hours, and his best plan was to venture out into the Chelsea dawn to clear his head. First, though, he made himself a cup of coffee, and even managed a slice of toast. He picked up Jet's folder lying on the table, and attempted to compare the bonus rates of different companies. Other pages told him the commission rates payable to the salesman. He was surprised how generous they were. All these mutual societies pooling the pennies of the poor were big businesses, sustained by the new business brought in by armies of salesmen. As a teacher, he would get a pension, and had no need of a pension plan or life insurance policy. What he did need to do was to save up for a house.

Walking along the river in the autumn sunshine, he reflected on his miserably low salary, with a long pay scale promising jam tomorrow. Now that he had bought a car, there was hardly anything left after paying rent for clothes and entertainment, let alone holidays. How was he to put anything by? He saw the trap his colleagues were all in. The application of ruthless thrift and the counting of every penny ensured they bought their houses and fed and clothed their children. But once they had reached the top of their pay scales, maybe getting extra allowances as departmental heads, inherited a bit, paid off their mortgages, collected something on the maturity of the with-profits policy they had been paying into for ever, they were unable to abandon their thrift. Their idea of a spend-up was the purchase of a bale of towels in the sales and some new dinner plates. Far from going on a round-the-world cruise, they had a package deal holiday in Portugal. Mr and Mrs Tourtel had bucked the trend taking their VW camper van to Italy, gathering mushrooms and edible fungi in the forest. But two teachers' salaries were better than one. Mrs Thompson exuded parsimony from every pore.

21

It was apparent to him just how much of a sacrifice it was for his father to have prised him and his brother out of Truro Grammar, transferring them to the King's School Canterbury, and how pointlessly counter-productive. He could now recall the social functions his parents went to, and his mother deploring the fact she couldn't afford a new dress. Following the installation of central heating and an overhead shower, paid for by his mother's legacy from an aunt, nothing had been spent on the house. Then there was his choice of career. It was all set up for him to be an articled clerk in a local solicitor's office on an extremely low wage, but with the promise of a high salary on qualification and eventual partnership. He had chosen independence, but it seemed as big a trap as the dark office with the smell of leather and pipe tobacco he had fled. He almost envied Jet who remained addicted to alcohol and casual sex, would spend every penny of his own and everybody else's money, and die tragically young of consumption. Perhaps not, since the invention of penicillin.

But it was a nice day. He found a coffee stall and treated himself to coffee and a sugary doughnut. His spirits were beginning to lift, undimmed by the thought that, when he had finally got his passengers home, some hard work on the ancient history front awaited him. What was the chance any of them would be awake? He knocked on the door, before remembering the key was conveniently left under the mat. Mark let him in. They were keen to get back, though Jet was determined they should start another drinking session, bearing in mind the pubs were only open from twelve to two. For once Percy put his foot down. They all had to get back and prepare lessons. Tim was looking forward to his mother's Sunday roast. Percy managed to bundle them in the car and drive back without getting lost.

Chapter Five

A Change of Lodgings

Percy's landlady didn't approve of the fact he hadn't told her he wouldn't be back Saturday night, and maintained she couldn't get to sleep wondering if he would wake her up on return, or rather the dog would with his less than friendly bark from the kitchen. She didn't approve of his request for hot water for a bath, when Sunday wasn't a designated bath night, but Percy was insistent.

It was Mrs Thompson who thought he looked unhappy on Monday morning, and when he said his digs were unsuitable, but with a car he could travel easily, suggested he had a word with Mr Townsend. Percy's ears pricked up at the suggestion, for he recalled the same suggestion from Mr Tourtel. Mr Townsend was the owner of property, having inherited a large house converted into flats. He and his wife lived in one, the rest were let for modest rentals to respectable tenants. There was, however, a furnished bed-sit, not normally let, but kept for visiting guests. He was welcome to rent it temporarily. Mr Townsend had remained indifferent to the joys of motoring, and struggled to school via bus and Greenline coach. He reduced the rent payable in exchange for Percy's promise of a lift at least in the morning. The flat had a shower, limited cooking facilities and a gas fire on a slot meter. "I daresay you might have supper with us occasionally," Mr Townsend advanced as a selling point, though Percy was petrified of the idea of dining with Mr Townsend, and fearful that Mrs Townsend might, like Mrs Russell, see him as a sympathetic ear. There was no phone in the bed-sit, but there was a public call box nearby. Percy didn't want to use the Townsends' phone, especially as Mr Townsend had said on no account were they to be treated as social secretaries. Percy said he would drive Mr Townsend home that evening to examine the premises, and would be able to move in on Sunday.

At lunchtime in the staff room, he gave a slightly edited account of the weekend trip to Chelsea, confined to the fact that they couldn't see the show until their membership had been approved, rather than commenting on the pub they had visited. Mr Tourtel deplored both stage censorship and the legal fiction of members' clubs which weren't that at all. Percy was a bit concerned that he was going to recite the constitution of Hurstwood Tennis and Golf clubs in support of his argument, but he changed tack entirely. It was as if male homosexuality only existed as an unmentionable vice, the practice of which was forbidden by law, as was its portrayal on stage; yet it was widespread, normal, and formed a major theme in the English literature A-level syllabus. Had Marlowe's *Edward II* been written today, it would have been heavily censored. Mind you, he wasn't convinced either Edward II or Piers Gaveston were in fact homosexual, this being invented by disgruntled noblemen who objected to the king's appointments; but some of the dialogue in the play was pretty steamy by any accounts. But he had to single out *To the Lighthouse* by Virginia Woolf, which explored the sexuality of the characters, and even asked questions like whether women could be truly independent in a male world if they were heterosexual. He couldn't imagine the examiners asking the question whether Mrs Ramsay and Lily Briscoe actually had sex or whether it was an embrace that didn't go quite that far. There was the decisive moment referred to in the book when Mr Ramsay and his friend, Mr Bankes, are walking together. They see a hen with its young. Mr Ramsay, says, "Pretty." This is the dividing of the ways in their friendship. Mr Ramsay is very solidly heterosexual, rather more so perhaps than his wife, who finishes her encounter with Lily Briscoe with the lines, "You must marry." Mrs Ramsay then tries to get the widowed Mr Bankes and Lily Briscoe romantically involved by sending them on long walks. The humour seemed to be over the heads of his upper-sixth English class. Percy wondered if there had been a dividing of the ways in both his friendship with Jet, and with Mandy. It was more to do with his innate desire for security and humdrum respectability in both cases.

Mr Rowntree then weighed into the conversation, rather unexpectedly. Cited in the *Pro Milone* was the case of the army recruit who killed an officer who was taking away or attempting to take away his *pudicitia*. It was treated in law as legitimate self-defence. The recruit preferred to risk capital punishment by killing the officer than to live with dishonour. Baxter, who was in his upper-sixth class, had said he didn't follow the logic. Surely, the recruit had been overpowered, the rape committed, and the officer was killed afterwards by way of vengeance. He didn't believe there was such a ferocious struggle at the time as to warrant murder in self-defence, and surely if the recruit had been penetrated at all, he would still have lost *pudicitia*, even though the perpetrator hadn't actually shot his load. Mr Rowntree had not expected there to be any discussion on these lines of text, and was outraged by Baxter's analysis. Even so, it had raised questions in his mind. What did his colleagues think?

"Perhaps you should ask Mrs Thompson her opinion," Mr Tourtel remarked, mischievously, "but I am inclined to agree with Baxter."

"I think Baxter is homosexual. You can tell by his facial expressions. So is that Tim Russell he goes around with. You must have met a few homosexuals at Oxford, Percy."

"I was not in any *Brideshead Revisited* set, I'm afraid, Mr Rowntree," Percy replied firmly, but dishonestly.

The bell then rang for afternoon school, discontinuing the conversation.

After school Percy met up with Mr Townsend, whose life was dominated by the need to catch the 4.15 Greenline, if at all possible, rather than the later one, which gave him time for tea in the canteen and for sorting what to put where, and how to get as many books as possible in his briefcase. Percy's landlady was now used to him not always being home in time for his cooked tea, which she would leave in the oven. Due to problems with the dog, her assistance was normally required to get the dinner from the oven in the galley kitchen to the formal dining room. She usually ate in the lounge from a tray, watching television. Mr Townsend's navigation was not the best. He had never driven in his life, and hardly knew even the routes the Greenline and the bus followed. Percy had his AA book and the London A to Z. The necessity to chauffeur the portly Mr Townsend was not the most encouraging of prospects.

But Mrs Townsend was charm itself. In a trice she abandoned her planned intent to berate her husband for sins real or imaginary, and thrilled to the prospect of entertaining this charming young man her husband had brought home. Whether she had ever had a career of her own or would like to work was irrelevant. Her husband's modest income had long been augmented by inherited property and rental income. They had had no children. Spending money came naturally to her. She sat on committees and was involved with causes. All these activities demanded an extensive wardrobe and regular trips to the hairdresser. She appeared to spend a fortune on flowers. At the same time, it was apparent their apartment was decidedly chilly, and its furniture, imposing. The guest apartment was most suitable. Mrs Townsend wouldn't hear of Percy's prompt return to his landlady's tea. She insisted he ate with them. She always cooked more than the two of them could reasonably eat, even with her husband's enormous appetite. She had made vast quantities of goulash, and expected Percy to eat his full share, which, in the words of the Prayer Book, was more than he could possibly desire or deserve. Mr Townsend was anxious to fill his glass with a fine wine, oblivious of Percy's need to stay sober for the drive home, or preference for cheap plonk. Mrs Townsend had soon discovered his broken heart, but assured him it would quickly mend. Percy agreed, despite inner misgivings, to take the room. He wouldn't be able move in on Saturday, however, as he was going on the coach trip to Canterbury Cathedral organised by Mr Tourtel. Percy was familiar with the cathedral from his time at the King's School.

Fate having placed Percy and Chris Allsop together for school dinner on the first day of term, he had continued to dine with her. She was a few years older than him, and had a poise and sophistication which contrasted with Mandy's immaturity. He had to admit he was sexually attracted to her, even if he didn't fancy his chances. It wasn't clear whether he suggested she came on the trip to Canterbury or she suggested it. There was one spare seat in which Mr Townsend had expressed an interest, but hadn't actually reserved. Chris was smart enough to get the eight shillings and sixpence into Mr Tourtel's hand promptly. That Chris and Percy dined together was already the subject of idle gossip. What neither knew was that Percy had already been nicknamed Jason, because he did resemble a picture of the Greek leader of the Argonauts. Someone in Percy's sixth form Greek class was planning a sketch for the school concert based on the story of Jason and Medea as set out in the play, *Medea*, they were studying. Even had they known, it wouldn't have stopped her attendance, which was also likely to upset Mr Townsend, if he decided he did want to go after all.

Chapter Six

Canterbury Cathedral

The coach was a forty-two-seater. Boys had booked thirty-eight places, with four staff members, Mr Tourtel, Mrs Thompson, Percy and Chris. But at the last minute, one of the boys, Henderson, had cried off, and his place was taken by Mr Townsend, who turned up huffing and puffing, and nearly missing the coach. He was rather like the uninvited bad fairy in the story, but the boy he sat next to, Henderson's friend, Wilson, was more resilient than his fellows, and seemed happy to engage Mr Townsend in conversation. Rapidly forgetting his first love, Percy was telling Chris his entire life story and learning hers in turn. She was naturally intrigued by his attendance at the King's School, where he lost his Cornish accent at vast expense, the viewing of which might enable them to get away from everybody else, provided Mr Townsend didn't latch on to them.

Mr Townsend regarded himself as the world's leading expert on the Reformation, as well as the conflict between Henry II and Thomas Becket; and was anticipating the historians would gather round him as their natural tour guide. Mr Tourtel was well informed on the background history of the play, which was commissioned by Dean George Bell for the 1935 Canterbury Festival; he was also convinced that T. S. Eliot may well have written a masterpiece of poetic drama, but had in fact mounted a very spurious defence of Becket, which was ambiguous in the least. In his eyes it was essential that they viewed the Trinity Chapel, where the shrine had been, in order to understand the fourth tempter's speech, as well as the North West Transept, known as the Martyrdom, where the murder had taken place. Chaucer's pilgrims to the shrine exhibited the full flavour of medieval life, with its mixture of piety, superstition and smut. For what were the Canterbury Tales, but medieval smut?

Percy had sung in the Cathedral and attended services there. It was in many ways the best part of his time at the King's School. He also saw a continuing line from Greek religion into Christianity. Some understanding of religion was essential to the study of art, music, literature and history; but at the same time, none of it was literally true. He quite shuddered when he remembered a Baptist Sunday school he had attended for a time as a child. Percy had envisioned taking some boys round and giving his own account of the cathedral before Chris had come along. Chris had her own recollections of a school outing to Canterbury cathedral, and was happy to revisit it.

The M2 hadn't been built in Percy's time at the King's School, and it was good to bypass the Medway towns. The journey was very quick. Although some notes had been distributed about the cathedral layout and what to look out for, it was obviously going to be an exercise in anarchy, as they formed their own groups. Percy and Chris found themselves with Tim Russell and Mick Baxter and some other rather arty types. Mr Townsend managed to gather a few of the weightiest historians, fascinated by his knowledge of the Reformation. Mr Tourtel and Mrs Thompson stayed with each other and a small party.

Percy suggested there was plenty of time, and he would lead his group round the King's School first. There was little or no change since his time there, perhaps not much change since its conversion at the Reformation from monastery to school. The chemistry between Percy and Chris was increasing minute by minute. This was their first date, and far too public. Chris suggested they all had coffee and a cake and a little stroll round the town before doing the cathedral properly. They exited via the Mint Yard Gate, and found a nice little café in Northgate. She got on famously with the boys, exercising control over the situation, and boldly insisted on picking up the tab, despite Percy's protestations. She was an independent woman, however slender her means. They walked along the Borough, Palace Street and Sun Street to re-enter the cathedral. They pretended not to notice some of the Upper Sixth with pints in hand outside the Olive Branch, clearly exhausted by culture. They went back in through the South-West Door, and Percy took them energetically to the list of archbishops on the corner wall by the North-West door. Cathedral guiding was something King's School boys had done in contravention of school rules to pick up tips. Percy was as qualified as anyone to talk. He rather warmed to his subject as increasingly Chris warmed to him. The boys were exercising the utmost discretion. He pointed out the stained-glass window of Adam, and alluded to the destruction of artefacts and stained glass at the Reformation and under the Puritans. He explained how the Victorians were anxious to refurbish the cathedral as evidenced by the war memorials and the decorated pulpit, a reconstruction of the one destroyed at the Reformation. He then swept the party round into the Martyrdom, where Baxter loudly yelled, "Unbar the doors." *Murder in the Cathedral* was coming to life, but an ancient virger seemed less than delighted, telling him to be quiet, at least when he went into the crypt. They were all highly amused, as the man shuffled off into the crypt. They decided, in consequence, to go upstairs first, where they ran into Mr Townsend talking about the picture of Charles I in the side aisle to an accompanying band of sycophants or mockers.

"Charles 1 upset Parliament because he believed in the divine right of kings, and had no use for a body which would limit his power. With Laud, his archbishop of Canterbury, moreover, he had attempted to re-introduce Romish ways into Anglican services. Both were executed. Life under the Puritans was grim indeed. A king was needed to counterbalance parliamentary dictatorship. The monarchy was restored. Charles II then petitioned parliament that his father be declared a saint and a martyr. This was done. He was the only saint to be declared by the Church of England, which had abolished saints in heaven as a class. In protestant theology the souls of all the saved go to heaven, but once there have no influence on God's mind, and are unable to perform miracles at their tombs. In the picture Charles is seen losing an earthly crown and gaining a heavenly one."

Mr Townsend then led his followers on to a nearby stained-glass window which depicted the three wise men tucked up in the same bed, fully dressed, for the purpose of receiving the same dream. He cleared his throat and looked expectantly, as if he had made a very funny joke, and all should laugh appreciatively, even if not uproariously. Mr Townsend was quite knowledgeable on the stained glass. They therefore joined his party for a bit, but finding his explanations over lengthy, drifted up into the Trinity Chapel, where the scene from *Murder in the Cathedral* was being enacted with the fourth tempter.

Percy was not as familiar with the play as those studying it for A-level, so only a few lines stuck in his head:

"Think, Thomas, think of enemies dismayed, Creeping in penance, frightened of a shade; Think of pilgrims, standing in line...

"The shrine shall be pillaged, and the gold spent, the jewels gone for light ladies' ornaments.

"You only offer dreams to damnation. You have often dreamt them."

The scene concluded with Mr Tourtel leaping into the arena, determined on his slice of the dramatic action: "Now is the way clear, now is the meaning plain; Temptation shall not come in this kind again. The last temptation is the greatest treason: To do the right deed for the wrong reason."

There was a general round of applause, especially from some bewildered visitors who weren't expecting such excitement, and from a guided tour, the participants of which clearly thought the unofficial entertainment was a great deal more interesting than what their guide had to offer.

It was important for Percy not to be seen holding Chris's hand, despite the irresistible temptation to do so. Spotting Mrs Thompson, rather dwarfed by her male entourage, he smiled, hoping she would say something, as he felt terribly tongue-tied and embarrassed.

"I used to come here with my husband who loved the stained glass. Look at the central diamond depicting the burial of Christ, with four surrounding stories from the Old Testament, said to prefigure it. There's Joseph thrown in a pit by his jealous brothers; Samson in bed with Delilah, revealing his hair is the secret of his strength, whilst the Philistines wait outside; there's Jonah being thrown out of the ship and being swallowed by the whale, look at his wonderful red shirt; and down below Daniel is cast in the lion's den.

Percy hadn't noticed theses detail during his years at the King's School, and found himself squinting, and admiring his elderly colleague's eye. Mr Townsend was now pointing out the details in one of the miracle windows where the forester almost chops his leg off, but is cured of all injury. Percy was on stronger ground at the tomb of the Black Prince. He died before his father Edward III. His young son succeeded as Richard II. His reign saw the birth of Middle English with Geoffrey Chaucer's *Canterbury Tales*, and the Wycliffe bible. The cathedral nave was also rebuilt during his reign in the perpendicular Gothic style. He quelled the peasants' revolt, doing what the Regency Council told him; later, he sought only to have his own favourites in his Council of State, and a tame parliament to grant supply. He exiled his cousin, Henry Bolingbroke, who returned from exile while Richard was in Ireland, deposed him, and starved him to death in Pontefract castle. Shakespeare's play draws attention to Richard's deposition as the cause of the Wars of the Roses. Henry IV, as Bolingbroke became, chose to be entombed opposite the tomb of his uncle, to express his apologies for all the long eternity their souls would spend in purgatory.

"Bravo," said Mr Townsend, "now here's a question. In what year did the Hundred Years' War with France finish, and what other important event took place that year?"

"1453, the sack of Constantinople, and shouldn't we compare and contrast Charles I and Richard II," piped up one of the historians who had been dutifully shadowing Mr Townsend.

"By divine right, perhaps," Chris Allsopp muttered sotto voce.

There was an almighty scrum in St Anselm's chapel, where heated discussions took place on whether William II had a red beard or a red face, was or wasn't homosexual, and whether his death stag hunting was murder or an accident. A conversation then broke out on the ontological proof for God's existence, as first advanced by St Anselm.

Chris and Percy broke ranks at this point, rather hoping they might quickly escape into the crypt, cloisters or anywhere, by themselves. Coming down the stairs, they made their exit by the Warrior Chapel, in search of a quiet place to eat their sandwiches. They had of course been seen, but weren't exactly followed. Percy seized control of the situation, grabbed Chris's hand firmly, and propelled his prize through the Christchurch Gate, up Mercery Lane, across the High Street, or rather Parade as it becomes at this point, and along St Margaret's Street and Watling Street into the Dane John Gardens. It was a beautiful autumn day. Absorbed in each other's company they didn't see Tim Russell and Mick Baxter walk to the far end of the park, equally absorbed, but slightly more observant.

Mr Tourtel and Mrs Thompson were eating their sandwiches in the garden by the Queningate, used by Queen Bertha those many years ago when she prayed at St Martin's Church, which, with St Augustine's Abbey, was due to be visited after lunch. Mr Tourtel was fond of pointing out that the Tourtel who married the creator of Rupert, and was resident in Canterbury till her death in 1948, was a third cousin once

33

removed, whom he never met. He was aware many boys called him Rupert, but didn't know he was also referred to as Tortoise, in accordance with the lines of the Mock Turtle in Alice in Wonderland. "We called him Tortoise, because he taught us."

Mrs Thompson always cut a comic figure, dressed so plainly as to belie any passion whatsoever, except for ablative absolutes, particularly sitting with Mr Tourtel, who had the same style of glasses and a face withered by smoking. Losing hair on top, he combed it forward, but was prone to stroke it absent-mindedly in lessons, as if trying to charm away the bald patch.

Mrs Thompson's marriage had been disappointing. Firstly, she had to get married, and secondly was compelled to be the breadwinner, reluctantly passing her child over to her parents in his earliest years. She had not properly bonded with young Robert, and her husband had shown little interest in begetting more children. He found work irregularly as a commercial artist. It was a rather loveless marriage. Mrs Thompson took to teaching in a boys' school, with secret infatuations on her male colleagues, increasingly disguised by her plain style of dress. Her big loves were chess and crosswords, and she found pleasant companions in these pursuits, though it was a pity her companions blew so much smoke over her.

She had always admired Mr Tourtel for what she thought was his slightly superior intellect as well as his Oxford degree. They talked in literary and classical allusions and quotations. She had been godmother to his wayward daughter, and was often a sympathetic ear. On the other hand, she had never become particularly friendly with Mrs Tourtel, who she usually met only at school plays. Mrs Thompson repaired the costumes sent by Nellie Smith Theatrical Costumiers of Nottingham, while Mrs Tourtel applied make up. In one sense Mrs Thompson was seeming to stab Mr Tourtel in the back, having perhaps failed to ensure his succession, but the headmaster always thought Mr Tourtel a bit incompetent, whilst being jealous of his intellect. The head admired ruthlessness, and hence admired Mr Rowntree. Mrs Thompson had no idea what to make of Mr Rowntree as a person, but he could certainly translate any piece of Latin put to him.

"How successful do you think this outing has been?" she eventually asked, after finishing her banana.

"I'm not really bothered," he said. "It just seemed ridiculous to study *Murder in the Cathedral* and *The Canterbury Tales* without coming here." He was about to animadvert on visiting sites of classical antiquity in relation to Latin and Greek, but refrained. Apart from a trip to Paris, Mrs Thompson had never been abroad. Greece and Italy had quite passed her by.

"I did try to get my husband to come, but first Henderson reserved the seat, then Mr Townsend took his place. Talk of the devil." Mr Townsend was sighted entering the garden at that point. They waved without enthusiasm.

"A messenger from Rome," they said in unison. Mr Townsend rather glowered. "Your Percy Spenser is moving into my flat tomorrow, but there'll be no hank-panky with that mathematician."

"Which mathematician is that?" Mr Tourtel asked in feigned ignorance.

"No good will come of it. Mark my words." Mr Townsend expostulated.

"Good luck to them," said Mrs Thompson. "I hope they have better luck than me."

In all her years at the school she had never commented on her marriage or her husband, except to suggest he was a bit lazy, like all men.

"A trip to Canterbury should be compulsory for all historians. The Reformation comes alive, the Middle Ages come alive." He sat down, and said he was going to smoke one of his occasional small cigars, offering one to Mr Tourtel, who lit up with pleasure.

"I buy them on my trips abroad, and a hundred usually last me a year."

"I'm afraid I get through a hundred cigarettes a week, as does my wife. But we do manage to cough our way round the tennis court."

"Perhaps that mathematician will be joining."

"At smoking or playing tennis? Will you accompany us round St Augustine's Abbey and St Martin's Church? We need a guide."

"I'm your man," Mr Townsend stated.

Meeting up for the coach going back, one could sense the vastly different experiences of those who had gone on the outing. For some the beer in the Olive Branch was uppermost. Others had fallen in love, or thought they had.

Chapter Seven

Moving In

Percy's mind was elsewhere as he loaded the car early Sunday afternoon to move into Mr Townsend's flat. He could think of nobody but, and nothing other than, Chris Allsop. He took several wrong turnings, and arrived some fifteen minutes after the approximate arrival time. Mr Townsend was less than friendly, but his wife was charm itself. After moving in, he had lessons to prepare. He hadn't done any shopping, and was about to set out in search of anything that might be open, when there was a knock at the door. Mrs Townsend brought him a loaf, some eggs, bacon and butter, and told him to have high tea with them, they having had their Sunday dinner whilst he was unpacking. "Take no notice of Mr Grumpy," she said, "Or discuss a historical topic." Percy said he would bear that in mind. High tea was an enormous salad with thick slices of meat from the midday roast, pre-buttered slices of white and brown bread, and a trifle.

Romance with Chris got under way at her lodgings where she was allowed visitors. They agreed not to consort at school, except at dinner. Chris would stay in the non-smoking half of the staff room, whilst Percy would endure the smokers' half, interesting himself in the chess game, or going out for a walk, should he need to buy some groceries. The drive in proved interesting. Mr Townsend was always lost in thought, but alert to the need to give a lift from the station bus stop to any school teachers not up to the final walk. In practice that meant Mr Ridley, whose leg arteries had been damaged by years of heavy smoking. He was of course always smoking a newly lit cigarette when they stopped for him, which he would flip extravagantly into the gutter. Percy had never seen such an ancient leather briefcase as Mr Ridley besported. "He's not the man he was," the other teachers would whisper, though his condition hadn't quite inspired them to give up the pernicious weed.

That first week at Mr Townsend's Percy attended a lunchtime debate, "This house believes charity begins at home." Framed innocuously as a maxim that leant itself to discussion, the hidden agenda was an attack on the school's charitable giving system. Each form chose a gift fund collector who was to go round extracting pennies from his classmates for storage in a tobacco tin and handing in at half-term and end of term to the master in charge. Statistics were then available as to which forms in each year had contributed the most. The headmaster believed in competition.

The proposers drew attention to the need to support first one's immediate family, then one's neighbours, then one's community, or one's church or grouping. True, one might have special concerns, such as the welfare of animals; but what on earth was the point of plucking charities out of the air for donation? The proposers were particularly scathing about disasters and famine and overseas aid. Large sums of money were collected, but no accounts were ever produced to see where the money had gone. There had to be a suspicion that funds were embezzled and diverted or wasted on the infrastructure of the organisations responsible for spending them. The donors were mugs. Had we not enthusiastically donated our pennies to World Refugee Year, without asking the reason for there being so many refugees? Had not vast sums of money already been spent in creating refugees, particularly in the case of Palestinians? In any event the sums people had to donate could be seen to be trivial, as if all the world's problems could be solved from school children's pocket money. How much does Great Britain still owe to the United States from the second world war? If you were contributing funds to build a scout hut, at least only finite sums of money were required, and you could be certain the funds weren't stolen. You were free not to donate, and one hoped the donations were not seen as an occasion for competitive giving.

The opposition took a different view. Charity was the most important virtue, exceeding faith and hope. It sprang from love and pity, and its purest exercise was in dispassionate giving. It was impossible to underestimate the good achieved by donations, and whilst it wasn't suggested people shouldn't contribute to the causes nearest to home, there was a need to be non-parochial. The Pestalozzi Children's Village was one such example. The charities were well run, and any paid officials received the most modest of emoluments. Charities for cancer research and relief were absolutely vital. In the days of the welfare state, we were in danger of leaving everything to the state and forgetful of personal responsibility. The speakers were particularly eloquent and somewhat theatrical.

The motion was thrown open to the house, when the issue of Palestinian refugees was brought up again. One speaker said that of course the Jews deserved a homeland, particularly after the holocaust, and Palestinian refugees were an inevitable consequence. Expenditure on creating Palestinian refugees was therefore entirely justifiable, but it was equally reasonable and indeed vital to donate for their resettlement, and not to agitate for their return as an alternative. A heated argument would have ensued if the chairman hadn't called an end to further discussion on that issue. Others got up. Boys were free to contribute or not to contribute to the gift fund, and should ignore the question of whether or not they were letting their classmates down if they failed to chip in. But nobody could gainsay the worth of donating to worthy causes, even if they weren't entirely close to home. One lone speaker thought the tobacco tin system was ridiculously unsafe. Funds should only be collected in tins the collectors couldn't open, and the money counted under proper supervision; but what could we expect in a school where the utmost importance was attached to collecting fraudulent marks for homework, in the apparent belief that competitiveness in form positions inspired boys to work harder? Another speaker stood up and said the motion could not be argued with. It merely said charity begins at home. It didn't say it begins and ends, or should begin and end at home; and even the opposition hadn't stated charity begins abroad. There were of course people, perhaps in a more bygone era, who had energetically given money to missionary work in Africa, whilst ignoring the poor on their own doorstep, and insisting their chimneys should only be swept by small boys forced to climb up them; but no one would hold a brief for them, or for slave traders who had founded hospitals. He suggested people abstain from the motion, which was ill-considered and meaningless. They weren't being asked to vote for or against the school gift fund.

The motion was defeated by seventeen votes to sixteen with seven abstentions.

The next two weeks were rather fraught: conducting the new romance in the utmost secrecy, chauffeuring Mr Townsend, doing for himself in the flat, preparing the ancient history lessons, steering the sixth-form Greek class through the opening scenes of the Medea, tennis coaching on a Saturday morning, and fending off Mr Rowntree's desire to play golf with him. It was perhaps a relief when the romance fizzled out. She was older than him, more experienced and needed a man who would assert himself. But whilst he felt they had both betrayed themselves, giving in to their immediate passions, she was only concerned with what the world thought. That was for her the only consequence. It was Wednesday 13th October when they finally split up, she told him not to cry, and kissed him one last time.

He agreed to play golf with Mr Rowntree that Saturday afternoon after his fifth morning tennis coaching session. He had been loaned a few clubs by the Russells. Jocelyn had more experience at the game, but Percy had a natural swing. As someone said to him, it was the tennis backhand stroke in reverse. Jocelyn was keen on getting into a club, and wondered if Percy might be able to assist. Percy hoped Jocelyn had no inclination about his connection with the Russell family, but whether he did or didn't, Jocelyn couldn't help animadverting, that Russell and Baxter were homosexual, being always in each other's company, though in different years. Percy refused to speculate, and would have fallen out with Jocelyn were it not for his position as heir to Mrs Thompson, who Percy liked very much. He had to admire her skill at chess, but wondered why her set didn't play bridge. Perhaps it was too difficult to get four together. He changed the subject to ask Jocelyn whether he played either chess or bridge. Fortunately, he played neither, and had no wish to.

There was soon some important news. A replacement had been found for Mr McKenzie, who would be coming next term. Mr Tourtel would lose some of his English classes and be able to resume some Latin ones. Mrs Thompson could now retire, but teach part time. Provided her teacher's pension and part-time salary did not exceed her full-time salary, it was in order. Mr Rowntree would take over as head of the classics department.

Meanwhile, a surprising literary opus turned up, indicating the presence of a poet and satirist among the sixth- form boys. It was a typed carbon copy which turned up in a pile of history essays. Mr Townsend who had thus received it was actually quite amused by the account of himself, and had no hesitation in passing it on, after ensuring a copy was made by the school secretary, who typed it up quite happily, with several carbon copies, but kept it secret from the headmaster.

A Canterbury Tale

When autumn comes and starts the new school year,
Both staff and pupils shake alike with fear,
If challenged by the reading of set books,
On which they cast their downbeat, gloomy looks.
No muse of poesy blows with inspiration
On staff or pupils at the railway station.
So Tortoise Rupert, smoking by the fridge,

Bethought it's time to make a pilgrimage,
To seek what palmers sought in Canterbury
From saints whose life was really not so merry,
And Thomas Becket was foremost, I wist,
Whose death King Henry ordered, shaking fist.
The blissful martyr's final resting nook
Is twixt the Black Prince and young Bolingbroke,
To where he'd lead the modern sixth-form class,
Hoping that something good might come to pass.
The north-west transept is the martyrdom,
Where Thomas' head was sliced to kingdom come.
His soul went up to heaven from our sight,
And you may pray to him by day or night.
And miracles he can and will pull off,
If only you believe and do not scoff.

Befell that in that season with good cheer
Within the Olive Branch, as I supped beer,
Me saw the Rupert troopers, all so merry,
From charabanc alight. They were not weary.
For swift the journey from the grammar school,
Along the new M2, the Pilgrims' Jewel.
No time for telling stories short or tall,
But I'll relate to you what did befall
Of some of them, so as it seemed to me,
My comments coming well to you for free.
Of Tortoise Rupert, I've already spoke
His snail pace in set books was a joke.
For him was always curious and thorough,
Though many thought he was not to the point,
And in the class pretend they would to faint,
And thereby get a part in his school play.
Excess rehearsals they were not his way.
But chose he pupils who could learn their lines,
And method acting treated with disdain,

Nor in the art room fashioned he costumes,
But they were hired from another's looms.
His wife applied the make-up with a trowel,
And happily ignored she many a scowl.
They had a daughter, Josephine by name,
In truth to them was somewhat of a pain.
Strange substance smoked she in the garden shed,
And listened to Bob Dylan when in bed.
In Engeland him wore thick woollen suits,
But when in Italy wore always shorts,
As did he on the tennis club's hard courts,
Where at the net he played formidably,
But afterwards was friendly over tea.
In company with him the classics head,
Elvira Thompson, all her cares had shed,
Delighted to be out for the whole day,
Not pouring cups of tea without much pay,
Or poisoned by the fumes of Exmoor Hunt,
Smoked in the staffroom by old Mr Lunt,
She checkmated so oft, when playing chess,
If he had not resigned. She knew best move,
And in her dress was always out to prove
She was no vamp; but ever so demure,
With long grey skirt, cream blouse and black bow-tie,
In no-one's eyes would she be any fly.
Set books she taught enthusiastically,
With chapters not selected by the board,
And made her pupils read more than they need.
Will do them good. I'm sure you are agreed.
She wore no make-up, never dyed her hair,
As if of her appearance not aware.
Forsooth she cut a slightly comic figure,
But oft for learning that is aye the trigger.
For pupils' interest is thereby aroused,
However dull the lessons said out loud.

With them was Turnip Townsend, bald and stout,
Of whose sports jacket few for joy would shout.
His trousers of the size of forty-two
Suspended were by braces long since new.
His shirt was tucked inside his underpants.
His boots so heavy were he could not dance.
Him was a very learned Oxford scholar,
With pockets holding many a U.S. dollar.
For his great wealth was really not a secret,
And all there was to know he really knew it.
Of history old and new and Byzantine,
Of music, art, religion, books so fine.
And at his own jokes he had ever smiled,
But many a boy had really got him riled,
When he'd get mad and rant and rave and shout,
Or purse his lips and then would flout and pout.
With affability he would not smile
And chased his trespassers full many a mile.
He ne'er indeed would simper graciously,
Or calm down slowly with a cup of tea.
But like a donkey, if his ears were lying flat,
'Twas then you might approach him for a chat,
And safe to ask to use the history room,
Where tournaments of chess would be no doom.
Him on the Greenline coach to school would ride,
For truth to tell he could not learn to drive.
Nor had his wife, who went to many a place,
In lovely dresses, made from finest lace,
And always in a taxi was she seen,
But not with him. My God, where has he been?
She would not roam around with such a fellow.
The thought of it would surely make her yellow.

With him his lodger, Percy, young and cute,

Y-clad from head to toe in chequered suit,
With locks so curly, as in rollers pressed,
For sooth at twenty-two his age I guessed.
And six foot one I think in certain length
And known more for agility than strength.
In blue and white his cotton shirt was striped,
And always neat his notes, but never typed.
Short was his gown with sleeves so long and wide.
Full oft his Morris Minor he did drive.
And in assembly sung that line so odd,
Extolling aye the panoply of God,
Containing as it did some words from Greek,
Which subject he did teach from week to week.
The thought of women made him pant and blush.
Like many lads he went from crush to crush.

A certain lady joined him on this trip.
Of scented fragrance, luscious were her lips.
A fiery red-head with a bee-hive cut,
Dark painted eyebrows from her face did jut.
In short, black skirt and sweater, roll-neck topped,
As coming from the dance floor she had hopped.
Chris was her name, and Percy she had met,
When in the dining-room annexe they sat,
And chatted over lumpy mashed potato
And other food that was so very so-so.
She well explained Pythagoras's theorem
To boys who only thought about her bosom.
Today she sighed for gardens in seclusion
To snog with master Percy in profusion.
In Anselm's chapel slipping entourage
As pricked them both nature in hir courage.

So many boys were also on the trip
Their varying details I can't let slip.

Though all were randy, quite obsessed with sex,
Espied me yet few love bites on their necks.
And wore they coats of leather with blue jeans,
Or pants of charcoal grey, with neatest seams,
And jackets quiet of colour and design,
And short white raincoats that did look so fine.
With innuendo peppered was their talk
That they each other's rears would like to stalk.
How they behaved when taking their school shower
Is not a matter for a decent hour.
Their schooling certainly was not co-ed.
They only thought of what to do in bed.
So I must end my story here and now.
A drunk voyeur, it's time to take my bow.

It was read and re-read eagerly, but no-one was quite sure who the author might be. Baxter was suspected, but he had shown no signs of poetic talent. It was thought the carbon copy had been leaked perhaps maliciously, and it might have been intended as an entry in the end of term informal concert.

Chapter Eight

The Fund of Funds

Percy's life was not proving any easier after splitting with Chris. The Tourtels were very absent-minded. He had been invited to come round after school to admire Mr Tourtel's collection of classical texts, commentaries and histories, if any would be of use to him, on the strictest of loans, of course. Some of the books in the collection were said to be valuable, but all were rare and out of print, lavishly bound and expensively repaired. He had left his car in the school car park, and walked the short distance along Covert Road. To his surprise, the door was answered by Josephine, who knew exactly who he was. "They've had to go to an emergency tennis meeting," she said, "but do come in." She was in forceful mood, rather as her mother was said to be when applying theatrical makeup. Percy found himself sitting in the infamous garden shed, which was exactly the ideal art student's room. He was soon drinking a cup of camomile tea. Josephine meanwhile appeared to have rolled a strange cigarette. She popped it in his mouth, despite his protestations about not smoking anything, and he felt almost instantly stupefied. It wasn't long before they were making passionate love. Percy had once been accused of resembling Mr Pooter, the alleged nobody, whose diary was published after extracts appeared in the magazine *Punch*. Whenever Mr Pooter took a glass of wine, it was always a thing he never did, which always resulted in a drunken escapade. So it was with the reefer and the love-making. But suddenly all was alarm. The Tourtels had returned from their meeting. Percy had to escape over the garden fence and get back to his car across the rugby pitch without being seen. He did indeed get back, climbed into the driving seat, and nodded off. A short while later, he was awoken by a tap on the window. It was Mr Townsend who had been staying late at school, with some society or other.

"Good you're still here, Percy. But has your day really been so tiring?"

Percy could only think of something half-way near the truth, hoping that corroboration would not be sought. "I had some of Mr Tourtel's blackberry wine," he said feebly, "with the addition of some fiery Italian spirit." Mr Townsend was resourceful. "I've a little black coffee in my flask."

Percy imbibed the coffee, and drove them both back, without incident. On return, he found a letter in a familiar hand. It was Jet's.

Hallo old thing. Guess what! I'm working for a decent company. They really value their salesmen, and teach you the art. "Do you sincerely want to be rich?" we ask ourselves. If yes, we must close the deal. The company's Investors Overseas, and run by a man called Bernie Cornfeld. We market single premium life insurance policies invested in US mutual funds, under a wrapper called the Dover Plan. Your Mr Townsend has filled in the coupon in the Daily Mail. Whilst taking a generous commission, I'm going to make him a millionaire. I would like to come Friday next week. So you'll put me up, won't you?

"Oh dear," thought Percy, "my half-term treat, a visit from Jet! Why can't life be simple?"

Mr Townsend had inherited quite a bit from his father, mostly in property, but there were some shares, and some property had had to be disposed of. It was true to say his funds were not terribly well invested, and he needed advice from someone both honest and shrewd. However shrewd, it was doubtful whether Jet would be entirely honest. He was out for his commission, after all.

Percy didn't want to get involved. He spoke to Mr Townsend confidentially, explaining that the allocated agent, Jet, had been a friend at Oxford, and asked if he might stay the night in the flat. He went on to warn Mr Townsend that Jet was a very plausible rogue. Mr Townsend thought it all rather fun. You and your friend should come to dinner, and he can see me Saturday morning in my study. The thought of seeing

Mr Townsend in his study on a Saturday morning was so frightful, Percy wasn't sure whether to laugh or quake in his boots. It would serve Jet right, but if he can sell this Dover Plan, good luck to him.

That Friday Jet was brilliant over dinner and in his cups. He painted a wonderful picture of his and Percy's time at Oxford, and of himself as coming from a privileged aristocratic background, and knowing any number of famous and titled people. Mrs Townsend was entranced. Why didn't she spend her time with such delightful and entertaining people, instead of being stuck with her boring husband, who did nothing but grumble? He moved on to investments, extolling the lucrative ventures the funds were invested in, and not zombie businesses going nowhere.

Percy and Jet were dispatched rather sooner than expected. The Townsends were early to bed and early to rise. Jet proceeded to get drunker and drunker back in the flat as they imbibed a bottle of green chartreuse. Percy was then completely unable or unwilling to fight off Jet's sexual advances, but in any event they both passed out immediately. Percy dreamed that Investors Overseas, or IOS, would turn out to be the biggest financial scandal since the South Sea Bubble, and that Mr Townsend would be ruined.

Somewhat predictably, Jet was unable to make a morning appointment with Mr Townsend, as they had risen early and departed to visit friends. Jet had, however, left them the paperwork to sign up, which they put under the door before they left. It was a relatively conservative sum that Mr Townsend committed to the venture, but the commission rate was extremely generous. There was little transparency on the charges, but much hype of the growth rate.

Percy managed to make the tennis club for his coaching session. When he got back, Jet was barely stirring, but he insisted Percy came to

London for the evening. Percy was only too glad to do so. The thought of a Saturday night on his own in the flat was too much.

Jet felt flush on the commission made from Mr Townsend. In the Colville that night he poured drinks down Percy's throat, whilst performing to a crowd he had gathered with ease his usual turn about all the rich and famous people he knew. Percy had long since suspended any belief whatsoever in anything Jet said, but had to admire his chutzpah. He was clearly a natural for the selling of dubious investments, and seemed to have been signing people up right, left and centre for the Dover Plan. Percy met Jet's elderly landlord, who, too, had invested a modest amount. It was mid-Sunday afternoon before Percy drove back, but he had avoided the temptation for a hair of the dog.

Chapter Nine

The Biggest Fraud of the Middle Ages

Percy soon forgot his worries about the fraudulent nature of the Dover Plan, when attending the debate "This house believes the canonisation of Thomas Becket was the biggest fraud of the Middle Ages." Debates on religion were always attended by the members of the Christian Union who almost out-numbered those otherwise attending. The Catholic Society had but one member, its founder, Hugh Bridge. There was a separate Catholic grammar school, in consequence of which there were few Catholic boys attending Hurstwood. They were obliged to skip the religious service in assembly and not attend R.I. lessons. None of them had ever felt the need for a Catholic Society, and detested being labelled as different. Some were even known to defy their priests and attend assembly, but you could get your homework done in the R.I. lesson. Bridge, however, was a convert to Catholicism, and valued the chance to debate both with the Christian Union and the atheist/agnostic sixth- formers.

The proposer of the motion stated quite distinctly that the assassination of Thomas took place in the Middle Ages; no one in the business imagined his soul had gone to heaven; no miracles took place at his tomb; the subsequent canonisation was therefore intended to make money from the pilgrimage trade; and no one doubted that Thomas's shrine was rapidly the richest. It was therefore the biggest fraud of the Middle Ages.

It wasn't quite clear what line the opposition were going to take. Bridge was the first speaker for the opposition. He believed in the death and resurrection of Jesus and in continuing revelation. It therefore followed that the souls of martyrs and exceptionally good and devout people went to heaven, and that they were enabled by God to perform miracles. Bridge deplored the reformation and the destruction of Thomas's shrine.

51

Protestantism was in his mind on a par with atheism. No one could prove that miracles had not taken place at Thomas's tomb. They were witnessed and recorded by two faithful monks, and set in stained glass. Pilgrims would never have gone to his tomb in such numbers if nothing miraculous happened.

The seconder for the motion professed himself to be a practising Christian, a member of the local Baptist church. He didn't doubt that Jesus had performed miracles, but no sane person could now believe miracles had taken place in Canterbury cathedral at Thomas's shrine. Pilgrims in the Middle Ages, however, would have believed in the miracles, because they believed what the Roman Catholic Church told them. Indeed, the words for pilgrimage and travel were the same. Shrines were places of special interest, because the Church had declared the occupant of the tomb's soul was in Heaven, in advance of the day of judgement; whereas the rest of dead Christian souls were in Purgatory, awaiting the return of Jesus, and only then, reunited with their body, would they ascend into Heaven. The medieval church was fraudulent and greedy. Whilst Henry VIII's motives were mixed, he was right to stop the worship of saints, the trade in relics and pardons, and belief in purgatory. These were fond things, vainly imagined, founded on no warranty in scripture, as stated in the thirty-nine articles. All Christian souls were in Heaven, but could not perform miracles at their tomb, or change God's mind.

The speech earned him a round of applause from members of the Christian Union, although the proposer looked rather bemused by his seconder.

The seconder for the opposition said that pilgrimages and indeed the pilgrim trade were unifying factors in society. This applied in both ancient Rome and Greece, as well as the medieval period. Pilgrimage could not be impugned on the grounds of naivete. The biggest fraud of the Middle Ages, as of today, was the necessity for war. War contributed nothing to the good of society, but cost infinitely more than pilgrimage.

The motion was then thrown open to the house. Speakers for the most part considered that all religion was fraud, and it was disingenuous to postulate that you voted for the motion as a Protestant, but against it as a Catholic. One boy argued that Christianity in particular, not religion in general, was the biggest fraud of the Middle Ages, and the canonisation of Thomas was merely a part of that fraud. It could not be a larger fraud in its own right. The argument that war or the necessity for war was a form of fraud was debated at length. People who went to war and raised money for that purpose usually had an honest if mistaken view as to the sense of their actions. They could only be fraudulent if they were lining their pockets. This was seldom the case. They always spent more on war than they raised from the taxes to fund it. The canonisation of Thomas and the necessity for war were not *ad idem*. The first was something that took place, arguably to make money by pretending miracles would take place at the shrine; the second was merely a concept.

Then someone stood up and mentioned the Crusades. Could these not be directly compared with the canonisation? The Crusades cost more money than was ever put on Thomas's tomb. The necessity for them, the essential virtue of them was fraudulently advanced to all and sundry, both those who went on them and those who paid for them. Everything about them was utterly shameful. The Crusades were the biggest fraud of the Middle Ages. There was a strong round of applause for this. The motion was defeated.

Chapter Ten

A Guest Appearance

A week later Percy returned to his lodgings to find a letter from his twin brother, William. Having studied fine art, William was now working perilously in London's west end in the gallery and auction trade. The brothers hadn't had much to do with each other since leaving the King's School, save for periodic appearances at the tennis club in Truro, where they never failed publicly to impress, and privately to quarrel. William had always been more successful with the girls than Percy ever had. This had given rise to a certain amount of rancour and jealousy, Percy thinking William aggressively chatted up the girls Percy was interested in, whilst ignoring his own admirers, until Percy switched attentions to William's admirers, when he too would promptly switch attentions. The twins were better apart, but the girls probably found the rivalry rather fun.

It so happened William had a piece of business to transact in Hurstwood, and said he would attend on Percy at the school. Percy was mildly distraught. It was preying on his mind during his ancient history class the following day. Driven mad by the sheer tedium of the text book, Bury's *History of Greece*, he found himself asking his class for advice. His class were unanimous. He should take his twin to attend the joint literary society meeting with St Bertha's, the local girl's grammar school.

"You're supposed to take a piece of poetry you like and talk about it. You could have written it or translated it. But not everybody has to have a piece. You can just be in the audience."

Tim Russell then volunteered he had translated a piece of a chorus in *Medea* into verse, which would be suitable. Percy had scribbled verse translations of extracts from Greek drama as part of his studies at Oxford, and thought one might do, if he could find it. The class were gratified by Percy's interest, which meant the possibility of a lift. Mr Duvivier, the English master involved in arranging the event, already had a full car, cramming six passengers into his Ford Zephyr with the bench seat in the front. Mr Duvivier always wore bright ties, and linen suits in the summer.

"I don't know who he fools, driving that car," as Mr Rowntree used to say. "Anyone can see he's one of those."

Hurstwood had a good turnout at the combined meeting, though inevitably outnumbered by the girls and teachers of St Bertha's. The extracts from Greek tragedy went down well, especially with Mr Duvivier. But there was a certain Miss Evans, an English teacher, who caught the eyes of the twins. Inevitably, William homed in on her, pre-empting his brother, but not for long. They were both spell-bound by her company, and she by theirs; but Percy had the advantage of greater geographical proximity, and besides, William was living with his girl-friend, which he was too honest to deny. By the end of the evening Percy had her phone number and the best wishes of his brother. William's business in Hurstwood had not been concluded, and it was agreed he would stay at Percy's overnight, transact his business in the morning, and attend on the school at lunchtime. He would have to be introduced to Mr and Mrs Townsend, but the chore would be allayed by fine wine, readily poured.

The following morning William got out of the car at the precise spot where Mr Ridley usually got in, promising to turn up at 12.35 sharp, when first lunch sitting commenced. Mr Ridley climbed in, after blinking in slight disbelief. William duly turned up at 12.35, and was escorted to the staff room, where Percy was anxious to introduce him to Mrs Thompson. The lady was already thinking about her chess move, and failed to express the interest she might have done, except to comment that their hair colour was as alike as that of Orestes and Electra, an allusion which Percy naturally picked up on, but William

55

didn't. Mr Rowntree came bounding over with the confidence and authority of a man soon to be the other's overlord, but was a little ruffled when William stared him manfully in the eye, on being told he was shaking hands with Josh Rowntree, and said, "I've heard so much about you." But had he?

"What exactly?" asked Mr Rowntree, fearful of any accusations of bullying. "Problems with golf club admission," William replied. "Why not try tennis?"

Mr Rowntree had failed dismally at tennis. His wife played, and might well have been encouraged to join a club, had her husband shown interest; but his idea of a sporting interest was one that would get him away from her apron strings. The idea that the Rowntrees should achieve social intercourse with the Tourtels on the courts and in the club-house was anathema to him. That it would have been equal anathema to them hadn't entered his head. He was perhaps dimly aware that the parents of his present and former pupils might have sat on selection committees, and had their own opinions on his teaching methods. To be a popular tyrant required charisma and cash. Ancient history might have taught him that much.

"I'm always hoping someone might pull a few strings. You must excuse me. I have further research to do on the Gracchi." As he moved away, Mr and Mrs Tourtel entered the staff room. She was on the scrounge, somewhat prematurely, for props for the end of term nativity play at her school, and a pantomime, which Mark Thornby and Mandy Russell were to be directing. But on the sight of William, she naturally moved in to book him for Saturday morning at the tennis club. He was unable to refuse, and promised to come down on Saturday morning for ten o'clock. She then swept off to the back stage store where she knew items were likely to be kept, if they weren't in the art room, with Mr Tourtel in tow, anxious to limit the damage.

It so happened that Miss Elizabeth Evans, or Liz to her friends, played tennis after a fashion, and had been invited along to the Saturday morning session. It was chancing it perhaps. Bonfire night had been and gone the previous week, and the fair-weather players had been dropping out. The juniors were lacking staying power and wanted to lie in bed on a cool morning. Older members, though in diminishing numbers, were still queuing up to partner Percy, even if he kept suggesting they played nearer the net. The twins played mixed doubles with Mrs Tourtel and Miss Evans, and then men's doubles partnering Mr Tourtel and the vicar. Miss Evans and Mrs Tourtel partnered each other against two rather sharp sisters, who took some beating. It was a successful morning. William took the train back to London and his girl-friend, whilst Liz invited Percy to come to see the school play, *The Zeal of Thine House*, by Dorothy Sayers, which she was co-directing. She described it as ambitious and unusual.

But the play wouldn't be staged for three weeks, and Percy wasn't sure whether he should contact her before. Was she Miss Right, he wondered, or another foolish crush? Meanwhile, he still felt guilty about the brief encounter with Josephine, whilst wanting to repeat it. It was so difficult looking the Tourtels in the face. Did they know, or suspect? He also hankered after Mandy, and thought fondly of Christine. It was still acutely embarrassing bumping into her in the staffroom.

He had only been with these three women, though there had been a number of chaste romances, with extended handholding. Some he had given up on, feeling he was being laughed at, or being offended at something trivial. In fact, lots of things Mandy did had grated, but the thrill had got the better of him. She wasn't the one for him, nor Josephine, nor Christine. Miss Evans came over to him as homely and virtuous in a way which suited his more puritan or old-fashioned instincts, but was this his imagination?

He really had no one to confide in, certainly not Mr Townsend, who had taken to confiding in him the secrets of the history department, on their journeys from school or when Percy had been invited in for a glass of wine. Mr Townsend was not the head of the history department, but merely head-designate, pending Mr Barmouth's retirement. Mr Barmouth had conceded too much control, he thought. The history department should control the teaching of economic history, but control had passed to the economics teacher. Then there was poor Mr Ridley, a shadow of his former self, due to severe diabetes and artery degeneration. He really wasn't up to teaching economic history to the fourth and fifth forms. The eleven-plus was a very blunt instrument. There was inevitably a bottom form of low achievers, whilst there were bright boys in the secondary modern. To make matters worse, there was always a shortage of maths teachers, despite our lady friend, and Mr Ridley was given third-form maths. Boys weren't ones to respect failing health, only to mock it. And, of course, ancient history should also be controlled by the history department.

Percy had taken the opportunity to say what he thought that history was best when you had original texts to read and compare, but historians kept quiet about their sources, and liked to think their text book was the final word on the subject. For the most part their text books, far from being works of literature, were dull beyond belief. "I hate Bury's *History of Greece*," he said in a heartfelt manner. "No spirit of enquiry, no quaint phrases, no jokes, no speculation, all done and dusted."

Mr Townsend had been surprisingly sympathetic. He had specialised in medieval history for its closeness to monkish chroniclers. He really hated the reign of George III, not something you were supposed to say. He had even asked about Percy's R.I. lesson with the question "How are you getting on with Genesis?" Percy had thought some of it was a bit naughty, but Mr Townsend had advised that sex was taboo, and those bits should be left out, but when they did Mark in the summer, he could read them Mark in the original Greek. Percy thought he could hardly convey the sound of first century Greek, nor did he see the point. The Authorised Version had quite sufficient majesty for all practical purposes, as well as being almost intelligible. Mr Townsend had rather liked the comment "almost intelligible."

The school's attitude to Religious Instruction or R.I. as a subject on the curriculum was quite extraordinary. To go by the strict formality of morning assembly with its hymn, collects, Lord's prayer and reading, the entire school were at least believing Christians, if not onwardly marching soldiers. The headmaster was known to be a Methodist lay preacher, and was indeed president of the much-maligned Christian union. One might have thought in these circumstances that R.I. O-level would have appeared on the timetable, but in fact there was one period of R.I. per week for every class, with no discernible syllabus. Mr Townsend oversaw the operation, and collected the extra allowance as head of the department. With two periods a week it could be taught to O-level, perhaps more successfully than economic history to the lowest stream. It was all the more interesting that the debating society's motion of Tuesday 23rd November was "This house believes school collective acts of worship and the compulsory teaching of R.I. should be abolished."

Percy duly attended, and found himself sitting with Mr Duvivier, who was the debating society's overlord. There was quite a good attendance with a full turnout from the Christian union.

The opening speaker for the proposition opined no rational person could believe there was some sort of super human in the sky who created everything from nothing, set up all the rules of maths, science and nature, and stringent rules of behaviour for human beings to follow, knew what everybody was thinking and doing, and indeed what the weather would be; and though capable of intervention in response to prayer, for the most part refrained from doing so, so as not to compromise our free will, or to teach us the deep inner resources we might learn through suffering and the testing of our faith, in the time of trial.

The idea that this super human being was obliged to punish everybody for failure to follow at all times such rules as were from time to time published by his agents, usually in stone, was absurd. Even more absurd was the idea that, to circumvent his own rule, he was obliged to be born of a virgin and undergo death by crucifixion. The incarnation and atonement were the most astonishing doctrines, let alone the resurrection of the body, the life everlasting, the communion of saints and the second coming. This was all unscientific, illogical nonsense to be expunged and eradicated in its entirety, and certainly not taught to the simple and gullible as solid fact.

The first speaker for the opposition emphatically denied he was simple or gullible, and drew a clear distinction between the high-pressure salesmanship of Baptist and other Sunday schools, and the low-key approach of official religion. Truth had nothing to do with it. Culture was everything, and so was singing, which was supposed to be enjoyable. What a pity, despite the best endeavours of the music master, and his inspired piano playing, school members made so little effort. No one could possibly be accused of singing their heart out. The more was the pity. Cranmer's collects were masterpieces of the English language, and how well the headmaster read them out, despite his smoker's cough. (*Laughter*) We all enjoyed reciting the Lord's prayer.

The bible was an integral part of our culture. What judicious selections were made for our edification by Mr Townsend, though their logic was not readily discernible. It was always exciting on a Monday morning to find out which prefect would be doing the readings, and what they would be reading. One did wonder why Mr Townsend kept the readings an official secret to four o'clock on a Friday afternoon or eight fifty-five on a Monday morning, but God moves in a mysterious way. (*Laughter*)

Assembly was insufficient to enlighten us to the full extent of our Christian heritage, and needed to be buttressed by a weekly R.I. lesson. He felt unable to comment on the value or worth of that further instruction, but the seconder to the opposition would doubtless take this up.

He stood down to loud applause.

The second speaker for the proposition had been listening intently and scrawling a few notes, primed to give a reply to the previous speaker, and not to stick to his original draft.

"Culture binds us with adamantine chains," he said. "We must break them. It is time to do away with the rubbish of past centuries. Haven't we had enough of the annunciation in our art galleries, along with all those fat Dutch women in yards of lace and flying cherubs?" (*Laughter*)

"What about the Inquisition?" he continued. "The church shamelessly opposed science, even to the extent of arguing, if the earth wasn't exactly flat, it was at least the centre of the universe, round which all heavenly bodies revolved. The book of Genesis was promulgated as scientific truth, and that therefore everything was created in the year 4004 BC or thereabouts. Religion has always been used as a tool of state oppression, and none more so than Christianity, the instrument to rob and enslave indigenous peoples, if not to wipe them out completely. Ethnic cleansing, forced labour, genocide, land expropriation and apartheid. All these have been the hallmarks of Christian culture, along with a compulsion to force orphaned and abandoned boys up chimneys.

"The speaker for the opposition was perhaps right not to comment on the value or worth of the further instruction received in what were referred to as scripture lessons in my junior school. All I can remember

61

of six years school R.I. is a term spent on minor prophets. We always took great delight in saying, 'Please sir, what's a whore?' A bit of sex education might not have gone amiss."

The speaker received a prolonged hand clap and loud cheers.

The second speaker for the opposition then stood up and argued boldly, "Gentlemen, ignorance is not bliss. It may very well be the case that God is going to punish people for not believing his holy word, and obviously they can't believe it, if they don't know what it is. It is therefore the proper function of the state to ensure its people do not reject God's plan of salvation out of ignorance. It is also a function of the state not to suppress the truths of its history nor the workings of its culture. The state has therefore rightly decreed that the school day should start with an act of corporate worship. Morning assembly is the opportunity for God the Holy Spirit to speak to each one of us and to accept Jesus into our hearts as personal saviour."

There were some groans of disbelief at this point from those who doubted either the speaker's sanity or sincerity, whilst a few cheers and claps from the Christian Union suggested some genuine support.

"The state has further decreed as the only compulsory subject on the timetable the teaching of R.I. We might not think much of what or how it gets taught here, or why it does not merit its study as the easiest O-level subject. But that is not the motion. We might well wonder why we do not have a school council in which pupils might be consulted about the curriculum. That might well be the subject for a future debate. No doubt, were there such a council, R.I. would be up for discussion. But there isn't. We are here to debate the legal provisions themselves, not how they might be more effectual.

"It is therefore my submission in reply to the proposers of the motion, that the corporate act of worship and the compulsory teaching of R.I. remain."

There was a round of applause, and then the discussion was opened to the house. Sensing perhaps that neither Mr Duvivier nor Mr Spenser were senior establishment figures, speakers followed their natural instinct for ridicule.

"*Honest to God*," said one senior speaker, pointing out that copies of this sterling work by the Bishop of Woolwich were purchased for discussion purposes by the headmaster's R.I. class, but unfortunately nobody understood a word of it. The book, however, sold very well, as did *Lady Chatterley's Lover*, which the bishop had recommended at its trial. Most of its readers bored themselves to death searching for the lewd parts. Of the two books, though, *Lady Chatterley's Lover* had the edge.

"Why is there a Bishop of Woolwich but no Woolwich Cathedral?" asked one wag.

The chairman pointed out that he was a suffragan bishop, and therefore didn't have a seat. Ignoring comments to the effect that that must make life difficult, the chairman selected the next speaker who stood up and said, "Gentlemen, we are so obsessed with exams that nobody can take seriously a subject in which they are not going to be examined. My R.I. teacher in year one said he had volunteered to teach the subject because he was a practising Christian. But even he gave up and spent inordinate amounts of time deploring how women, and in particular his wife, never stopped talking."

The next speaker animadverted that for pure time-wasting you had to hand it to the English staff. Discussion on the essay topics was the excuse for the English master to sound off about anything, but it was better than work, and highly entertaining. Mr Duvivier, who was one of the worst offenders, smiled.

The next speaker returned to the subject of sixth-form R.I. The year was split into two groups, one for R.I. with the headmaster, which was usually a discussion on anything except religion, despite the suffragan Bishop of Woolwich, the other for R.I with Mr Townsend, in which he played music, and not even church music. It so happened that Mr Townsend had been delivered the reports appropriate to the headmaster. He had commented on at least half a dozen before the mistake was realised. The speaker advised he was highly amused to see the comment "he should contribute more to discussion" crossed out and replaced by "Good."

The only Indian boy in the school was next to speak, who thought there should be a multi-faith approach. A Christian education was an imperialist one, which liked to think everything was invented in Western Europe. Grudgingly, it referred to Arabic numerals, but these were in fact Indian numerals. As for the Zoroastrian influence on Judaism and Christianity, we had to be content with the guest appearance of the Magi in Matthew's gospel. The Church of England was the Conservative party at prayer, and school assembly merely mirrored this. He got quite a round of applause, though it fell short of a standing ovation.

The final speaker stated he was a Christian, but believed in freedom of choice. The compulsory nature and derisory quality of school worship and R.I. teaching rendered it unacceptable. It was rightly treated as a joke.

The motion was narrowly defeated. The popular sentiment was that, though most boys were hardly interested in the Christian religion at all, the R.I. lesson was a welcome break in a crowded curriculum, some sort of assembly would be necessary, and there were those who enjoyed the singing. Indeed, the school choir was said to be a hot bed of atheism.

After this debate Percy wondered whether he had been taking his R.I. lesson with his form too seriously, and might have exercised a counselling role, as their form master. The odd five minutes, perhaps, he thought, but where would it end if he abandoned the reins? He might happily have taught them some classical mythology, but in point of fact the book of Genesis was worth knowing, even if not a word of it was historical truth. He thought he had struck a good balance between telling the stories himself and forcing the boys to read out the text. Their ability at reading out loud was poor, with some notable exceptions, who merited parts in school plays, but were unlikely to get them. He recalled his primary teacher in Truro, Mr Penhaligon, who turned most of his lessons into drama, until sacked for failing to teach any arithmetic. Percy's maths had never quite recovered.

Meanwhile, Mrs Thompson thought the Classics Department should have a brief get together on the plans for the following term. It seemed Mr McKenzie's replacement had been selected, but would not start till next term. Mrs Thompson had served forty years as a teacher, and though not obliged to retire till the age of sixty-five, could not add to her pension. She was therefore entitled to draw her pension, and work part-time, provided her combined pension and teaching income did not exceed a full salary. Mr Tourtel would be released from much of his English teaching. She could now become part-time and cede the department headship to Mr Rowntree, whose appointment had been decreed by Captain Turpin. They held the meeting the following day in the canteen where tea was served to staff members at four o'clock. Mr Tourtel was inevitably a little sulky, Mr Rowntree smug, Mrs Thompson a little apologetic, but looking forward to pub lunches in Blackheath with her husband on her days off. Percy's mind was on Liz Evans.

Chapter Eleven

End of Term Productions

The Zeal of Thy House by Dorothy Sayers, 2nd to 4th December, was perhaps an odd choice for a school play. It certainly wasn't chosen by Liz. It was the choice of the headmistress, Miss Webb. But as it needed a little assistance from a distant choir singing in Latin, Miss Webb had recourse to Liz, as music teacher, to become the musical director. Liz was soon promoted to director when Miss Webb found herself unable for unspecified domestic reasons to devote as much time to its direction in after-school rehearsals. The belief was that Miss Webb's mother was getting a little forgetful, as another teacher said to Liz in a confidential tone. Liz had taken to direction like a duck to water.

The play complemented the trip to Canterbury Cathedral. In 1174, four years after the murder of Thomas Becket, the cathedral quire, which had been constructed over a new crypt, was gutted by fire. A French architect who had worked on Sens Cathedral, the first complete cathedral in the early Gothic style, was commissioned for the rebuilding of the quire, and an extension to the crypt to support an extension to the quire, the Trinity Chapel, intended to house the shrine to St Thomas. Known as William of Sens, he slipped from some scaffolding, or fell when the rope of a crane broke which was winding him up in a cradle. It was suspected that he had been having an amatory liaison with one or more of the ladies married to someone in the cathedral circles not bound to celibacy, and that the accident resulted from the malicious act of a cuckolded husband. The chronicler, Gervase, recorded that the accident was the vengeance of God or the spite of the Devil. The detective story writer, and high church woman, Dorothy Sayers wrote the play for the Canterbury Festival of 1937 in verse, much as T. S. Eliot had written *Murder in the Cathedral* in verse for the 1935 festival.

In her version, William, who has been taking a few commissions from suppliers, becomes heavily involved with wealthy widow Lady Ursula de Warbois, but it is the Archangel Michael, seen by a young boy, who cuts the rope on the crane in 1177. William was paralysed by the accident, and though he attempted for a while to direct operations from his sick bed, gave up, returned to France and died in 1180.

Percy thought the entire sixth form studying English or history might have wanted to see the play, but there wasn't much enthusiasm. The Tourtels regretted prior engagements. Tim Russell and Mick Baxter wanted to see it. It didn't suit Percy to have to give them a lift there, so he was grateful when Mr Duvivier announced he was going and offered lifts to Tim and Mick, the only boys wanting to see it. Some of their friends questioned whether they would be safe, but Tim said they had the utmost confidence in Mr Duvivier's driving.

The production was extremely good, but the play was only a qualified success. It was a bit odd, too religious and over the heads of the audience.

The end of term treat most looked forward to in the run up to Christmas was the informal concert held on the Monday afternoon in the last week. Licence was given to boys to lampoon the teaching staff. Mr Duvivier was in charge, and whilst he was supposed to seek permission for more controversial entries from staff members affected, frequently forgot to do so, or else specified cuts were restored. Lower-sixth modern presented an item for which Percy's consent had not been asked, based on the plot of *Medea*, the set book he had been leading the Greek students through. The author was Tim Russell, and it was wickedly funny. Percy's nickname was already Jason, and as a parody the sketch didn't need much explanation. It was in the form of an opera. The story was as follows. Turnipus is the usurper king of Corinth, having killed Jason's father and sent Jason to exile in Bolerium. But now he has heard that Jason has grown to manhood and is returning. On Jason's return they submit the matter to the goddess Athena, who appears magically, and looks remarkably like Mrs Thompson. She says Jason must go across the Black Sea to Blackheath, and get the golden board duster from King Smarticus. She says he will give it in exchange for Jason's help in getting him into the golf club. Despite being king, they won't admit him. The goddess promises to help Jason.

He builds a ship called the *19th Hole* and gets a crew. On arrival, he leaves the crew with the ship and goes alone to meet Smarticus. Smarticus points a ruler in his face, and asks him to give the principal parts of to play golf. Jason says there is no such verb in Latin, and how come he can't get into the local club? Smarticus says he has to play off a three handicap, before they will consider his membership. Jason suggests they play on the public course, Smarticus fills out a low score card and Jason countersigns it; but there's no public course. Smarticus then says he will have Jason killed, and casts him into prison. In prison he is visited by Smarticus's daughter, Medea, looking remarkably like Chris Allsop, who says she will help. She has had a magic cabinet made which can temporarily change you into someone else. She will persuade her father to go into the cabinet and be turned into famous golfer Arnold Palmer for the purpose of playing to a three handicap. Smarticus goes into the cabinet, and someone dressed as a professional golfer emerges. He goes off for the golf test. There is a loud bang off stage and a messenger comes on to explain how Arnold Palmer turned back into Smarticus at the end of the ninth hole, and Smarticus couldn't keep up the play. The messenger advises them to escape. But first they need the golden board duster. At this point he prays to Athena, and another messenger comes on with an advice note that says Medea must go into the cabinet, and be turned temporarily into Athena. She will have the power to charm the dragon. This is accomplished. Athena turns back into Medea, and the cabinet then becomes a space travel machine in which they fly back to Corinth.

They are welcomed back, but Turnipus prevaricates, and says he has to perform various tests like guessing the readings in assembly. Medea takes Mrs Turnipus on one side, and says if she puts Turnipus in the cabinet, he will lose ten stone. She demonstrates with a large cuddly toy, that is reduced in size. Mrs Turnipus duly gives her husband a sleeping pill and puts him in the cabinet. Alas, a very slim and dead person emerges. An enraged Mrs Turnipus then declares counsellor Tortellius as the new king. She also pushes Medea in the cabinet. Athena emerges, and the change is permanent. Percy and Athena sing "Me and my Shadow," then Percy says he won't marry her, but will marry Tortellius's daughter, Tortellina. The daughter looks exactly like Medea.

Preparations for the wedding are underway, but Athena/Medea deplores her desertion and vows revenge. She gives Jason a gold acid-soaked dress for his new bride. Tortellina puts it on, staggers in horror and collapses. Tortellius rushes on, clasps her, and also collapses.

"What have you done?" Jason deplores the deeds of Medea, but she then says she's retiring. She goes into the cabinet, and Smarticus emerges waving a ruler in Jason's face and saying "Get me into the golf club, if you know what's good for you."

The sketch was very rough and ready, and the songs rather indifferent, but on the whole, it was a popular and daring piece. The actors who mimicked Chris Allsopp and Elvira Thompson had good costumes and wigs. Whilst both Percy and Chris were acutely embarrassed, the humour relied on the age and fashion differences of the two women teachers more than allegations true or false of sexual activity between participants.

A similar sketch emerged from upper sixth modern. It was entitled *Pro Smartico* or *Murder on the Appian Golf Club*. Smarticus is accused of murdering Testudo. Set in the Roman senate house, a boy imitating the headmaster was making the defence speech. Percy remembered this much: "My client is the bravest of men. Undeterred by delicacy or danger, he stands up to the smallest boy, boldly pointing a ruler in his face. Engaged in his defence, therefore, my timidity shames me. I do not see my wife handing out the medals to grateful competitors in the Games. Rather, my eyes are terrified by the sight of members of the golf club standing prominently to attention, where spectators normally sit, their caddies weighed down with drivers, seven-irons, mashies, putters and wedges, ready for use as weapons.

"If ever a man was so lucklessly charged with murder, it was Smarticus. The defence will show he acted only in self-defence, and therefore in accordance with all the laws. Supporters of Testudo have sought to deny Smarticus a fair and proper trial with their intimidation, but the facts remain.

"Smarticus was hoping to be elected to the golf club, Testudo had absolute sway over the committee. Testudo was hoping to be appointed Tribune of the Classics. Smarticus was favoured for the post by the *Magister Ludi*. Testudo knew Smarticus would have to take a short cut across the golf course, unopposed by the secretary, who was said to take a large snifter at that time, not to be late for an appointment with the chief Vestal Virgin. Testudo set an ambush by the sixth hole, concealing his troops in the rough and the woodland, pretending they were only going to push him in the water hazard, but in reality, to take away his life."

The defence speech got wilder and wilder, with layers of corruption levelled at all and sundry. It was a very clever parody of the speech that Mr Rowntree had been ploughing through with the Latin Upper-Sixth, formerly assigned to Mr Tourtel.

Percy did wonder how Mr Rowntree would take this criticism.

There were enough other sketches to divert full attention from the classical entries.

Afterwards, Mr Rowntree pretended to be amused, but when Mr Barmouth asked if he was thinking of changing his teaching methods, bristled, and said, "I don't know what you mean." Percy had his own impersonation to fend off with his pupils, and was hardly able to discuss his colleague's.

It was not the school's habit to have a Christmas party for either boys or staff. There was the Christmas carol service on the Tuesday afternoon, endured rather than enjoyed, following which a few mince pies and bottles of sherry were smuggled into the staffroom, probably rather fewer bottles than were normally stacked on the top shelf of the headmaster's steel cabinet; this was hardly the precursor to Bacchanalian frenzy. That year's proved no exception. However, whatever obfuscation resulted from the inferior sherry, all eyes were upon a certain Mr Sweet making his appearance as the new English teacher. He had a pronounced Scottish accent, though entirely comprehensible, and wore a houndstooth jacket with grey flannel trousers, a dark brown shirt and green bow-tie. He was escorted round the staffroom in a rather haphazard fashion by Mr Lunt, the English head, and Mr Duvivier, Mr Lunt displaying an amused tolerance, and Mr Duvivier, an uncertain fascination. He told everybody he wrote poetry, which is always a mistake, and admitted to having played Lady Macbeth. He also professed knowledge of Zen Buddhism and differing schools of yoga. "Well, why not?" said Mr Tourtel, knowing a small ceremony was about to take place, in which Mrs Thompson passed on the baton to Mr Rowntree, but remained teaching part time. The ceremony would officially acknowledge his being passed over. The experts were working on the revised timetable. Mr Tourtel's one trump card was to give Mrs Thompson a volume of Sophocles from his antique library. Mr Rowntree could hardly beat that.

Chapter Twelve

Earls Court and Truro

Term finished on the Wednesday afternoon after school dinner and a short final assembly. Percy could remember a time in his childhood when school holidays equalled bliss. Even the long summer break was hardly marred by the lost companionship of school chums, that feeling of unwonted idleness, or desire to be away somewhere really exciting, or at least different. His hatred of his school days, and particularly the King's School Canterbury, was so profound it expelled all other considerations, rational or not. Oxford had, of course, been an entirely different matter. Oxford equalled bliss. Back in Truro he was usually bored stiff, resentful of his mother's influence on him, and possibly working in some demeaning vacation job; or worse still, the alternative to Truro, thumbing a lift beside French roads, and sleeping in cabbage patches. What absolute anathema it all was. But the dynamics of this vacation were entirely different. He really did need a break. What a strain it had been driving Mr Townsend to school, whose grim morning humour so sharply contrasted with his nocturnal alcoholic bonhomie. Fine wine had a lot to answer for. Percy's father enjoyed a few pints most evenings in the local ale house, but was always either sunny in the morning or at worst slightly subdued.

Miss Evans was uppermost in his mind. Somehow, he thought she was playing with him, her attitude being casual or non-committal, which had quite inhibited his instinctive passion on their dates. But then she would say or do something quite mesmerising, as if to lure him back into her flame. He was then quite surprised that she invited him to come and stay with her and her parents in Bath for the New Year. He could hardly contain his excitement, accepting instantly and impulsively, and was then consumed with a nagging doubt that maybe her parents were expecting her to bring a nice young man to meet them, that she wasn't

72

really interested in him, and he was to be a virgin sacrifice on the altar of respectability. He shut these thoughts out as unhelpful and unworthy.

Meanwhile, there had been the inevitable phone call from Jet, summoning Percy for one long bender. Percy doubted whether his wallet or capacity were up to the vast number of drinkies that Jet had in mind. But somehow at the end of the day Jet was Percy's only friend, however badly he had behaved; and also, Percy suspected, he was Jet's only real friend, despite the extensive circles Jet mixed in. Nobody could accuse Percy of mixing in extensive circles, or even rarefied ones. His mother was convinced her husband was not just a drunkard, he was a chronic alcoholic, and the twins were emulating him on a slippery slope. His mother was known to hold her drink rather badly, which enlivened the occasional cocktail party she attended, when not sticking remorselessly to orange juice and lemonade. Mother masterminded all the paperwork, admin and accounts of the practice, without which help the twins could not have continued at the King's School, the credit for which she expected on a regular basis from all around her. Her bridge friends were accustomed to hear what she had done for those ungrateful boys and ungrateful husband, and nod in feigned approval, as if they hadn't heard it all many times before.

It seemed easiest to travel to London on the train Wednesday and stay the night. It didn't help that Jet didn't seem to know where he was living. His tenuous stay in Flood Street was coming to an end, and he was in the process of moving in with his new lover, Dominic Ward-Smith, who occupied what proved to be a rather squalid bed-sit on the Earls Court Road. Somehow Percy found his way from Earls Court station, and negotiated an uncertain entry phone and several flights of stairs. Dominic was clad in leather and denim, his hand was tattooed, and his luxuriant ginger beard was trimmed to exactly three-quarters of an inch. All Percy's attempts at beard growing had proved unsuccessful, but that was no reason to envy Dominic. Percy was reluctant to ask such obvious questions as the nature of Dominic's employment, but Dominic soon volunteered that he ran an after-hours drinking club with a supper licence. His chief function was to fend off all enquiring after the owner with demands for unpaid bills or protection money. The club went into insolvency quite regularly and re-opened under the same management. There was a members' list, regularly removed for inspection by the police. With membership fees, entrance fees, an over-priced supper and watered-down double gins, the club would have been highly lucrative, were it not for the depredations of protection money paid to gangs and police alike. It didn't seem to Percy that Jet's involvement with Dominic was something he could really condone. But Dominic talked smoothly without bragging and seemed to deserve the benefit of the doubt.

Jet arrived at the flat after a while with carrier bags of groceries and wine bottles. Despite coming straight from work, he was wearing a leather jacket. Jet assured Percy he now had a new job relying on his mathematical skills to conduct a detailed evaluation of balance sheets to determine whether the shares in the companies were worth buying. "It's the cutting edge," he informed Percy grandly, and then deplored his departure from the Dover Plan, muttering about fraudulent valuations. It wasn't clear who had fallen out with whom, or whether it was mutual. There was also another issue, recovery of his possessions from Flood Street. Percy was supposed to have brought his car, so they could drive round to Flood Street when the owner wasn't there to collect Jet's worldly goods. Exactly where Percy could have parked in Earls Court was a point that Jet had overlooked. Percy suggested they all went over in a mini-cab, and Jet could determine whether they might keep the driver waiting, or pay him off, and in due course get a black cab back. Dominic wasn't sure whether there was anything of value left in Flood Street, and Percy could dimly recall the same suitcase being regularly transported between Oxford and Jet's parental home without ever being opened. Its contents remained a mystery. Discussion took place over a bottle of wine and a rather salty spaghetti Bolognese prepared by Dominic, who liked to think he was a master of haute cuisine.

The resultant plan emerging from heated discussion at the meal was pretty much what Percy had first suggested. They would all go over to Flood Street in a minicab, and ask the driver to wait. Jet still had a key, and could hopefully gain admission and secure the suitcase. If he could emerge with said suitcase, Dominic would go back in the cab to Earls Court with it, whilst Jet would go with Percy to the Colville. If the owner were in, Jet could still get the suitcase, but it might take longer. Whatever happened, Dominic would have to get back to Earls Court. It was all the usual drama. Fortunately, the owner wasn't in, and Jet re-appeared with the ancient leather suitcase. He was intending to leave the key with a note, but thought another time might do. Dominic departed in taxi with suitcase, and Percy and Jet found their way to the Colville. It was still relatively early, and Percy thought they might get a proper conversation in; but after the opening salvo of "I'm in a new affair, but I don't really want it; and I have to do everything Dominic says; frankly I'm terrified of him," Jet spotted a friend and was in performance mode, leaving Percy to wonder. He found the pub rather interesting. For all that it was a stamping ground for those whose activities were criminal offences, or mortal sins, the clientele were predominantly employed in respectable bourgeois occupations. There was a very middle-class, grammar or public-school ambience. If only they didn't all smoke so much. Percy's eyes were soon stinging. Jet suddenly looked at his watch, announcing it was time to get to Earls Court. They were soon outside in the cold, breathing in air as fresh as it could be in the King's Road, Chelsea, late in December. Jet was well practised at hailing cabs, a habit too expensive for Percy to have acquired much skill at.

Between the Earls Court Road and Warwick Road on either side of the Old Brompton Road were two pubs of ill repute, the Boltons and the Coleherne. Jet explained that the Boltons was rough trade and rent, whilst the Coleherne was leather, which didn't mean anything because it was a middle-class fancy-dress affectation, though the odd motorbike was to be seen parked outside. Thus assured, Percy followed Jet into the hot smoke-filled bar. There was never anywhere to hang a coat. Perhaps that was why leather was so popular. Mind you, in Oxford a sports jacket and scarf were deemed suitable pub wear on all but the coldest or wettest of nights. Jet was instantly popular wherever he went. Perhaps he was good at pretending to know people and plunging into conversation. But any serious conversation or confidences seemed to be out of the question. It was very packed, and thus rather a relief at closing time, when they were forced outside onto the pavement, where there was much loitering with intent. Jet soon bundled him down into a nearby basement, the premises of the Night Porter club.

They were duly let in by Dominic, and found their way into a dark corner, where they hung their coats on the back of some chairs. It was here that Jet purchased from a passing stranger what were sometimes described as purple hearts. Percy declined pointedly either to purchase or consume any. Jet seemed unfazed, but to Percy's knowledge Jet's consumption of stimulants/depressants at Oxford had been limited entirely to alcohol. A waiter came round to take their order for snacks and drinks. The place filled rapidly, and the small central floor was packed with non-contact dancing. A rather strange smell hung round the approach to the toilets, which Jet informed Percy was amyl nitrite or poppers. These gave the user an instant erection. Percy really was naïve about all this. In Oxford he had perhaps been aware that Mandy's friends occasionally smoked illicit substances, but he had always preferred not to notice or certainly not enquire into what would not do him any good, with the reservation that tobacco was the worst of the lot anyway. His eyes had been stinging all evening. Josephine Tourtel had been a one-off experience in every way.

Sensing that Percy's thoughts were in the distance, Jet gave him one of his winning smiles, but then immediately turned the charm on a Spanish gentleman, who sat at their table and looked amorously at Percy. Percy wished for one moment he wasn't desperately looking for a wife, but into one-night stands with anyone available. The waiter brought them their unidentifiable snacks, with ill-tasting white wine, whilst the Spaniard continued in very broken English his account of life in a hotel laundry. It sounded pretty grim. Meanwhile, Jet's imagination was beginning to wander a bit, as he informed Percy of the celebrity identity of quite non-descript people on the dance floor. The trouble was Percy hadn't heard of as many celebrities as Jet had. The names and the faces meant nothing. He smiled and said, "Really!" by way of a put-down, but was instantly imitated by the Spaniard, who said, "Really, will you dance," and pulled him up. On the principle, "when in Rome, do as the Romans do," Percy danced, but tried not to look too interested. The Spaniard seemed to take the hint, but perhaps didn't quite get the circumstances right. He suddenly said, "I see you are in love with your friend," and disappeared into the crowd. Percy returned, and was somewhat amazed when Jet told him the Spaniard was really a spy for the Spanish secret police, reporting on the political affiliations of Spaniards working in England. Percy wondered whether Jet had got this idea from Percy's account of his own vacation work with Spaniards, but didn't pursue it. They had a few more drinks, and then it was closing time. Dominic would follow them back later. They walked back down the Earls Court Road. Everything was shut, even the Kentucky Fried Chicken outlet.

Back in the flat Percy insisted Jet opened the old-fashioned leather suitcase, the subject of the recent campaign. It contained sheets, table cloths, napkins, text books, exam notes, cutlery, jars of home-made jam, cricket whites and a penguin suit. Jet removed the remains of the earlier meal, and spread one of the table cloths out over the table. It looked better. He then stared at Percy and said dramatically, "Take me away from all this."

"I don't think you'd last five minutes renting from the Townsends, Jet," Percy said firmly. But if you're not happy with Dominic, I'm sure there are other squalid dives available in convenient locations."

Jet rather liked the "convenient locations" as an expression, and suggested Percy fried some eggs or made an omelette. Percy cast his eye round for ingredients and utensils, whilst Jet opened a bottle of Moroccan red from the local corner shop. Dominic arrived back, and their late-night supper continued with more wine. They told Percy they would not be offended if he left early without waking them up to say goodbye. He curled up on the ancient settee, whilst they continued chatting.

He woke up the following morning, irritated by the smell of smoke and fancying he could detect the smell of poppers, lingering round the flat. He had actually brought Jet a Christmas card, which he left on the table. Following the briefest of ablutions, Percy felt unequal to the task of making tea or coffee, and headed out into the Earls Court Road. On entering the Wimpy Bar, he noticed someone waving to him energetically. It was the Spaniard, Manuel, from the night before. Percy sat with him and was regaled with much the same story he had heard the previous night. Life was not quite as grim in England as it was in Spain, but it was a shame about the weather. Manuel enquired as to Percy's plans for Christmas, and on learning he was going to stay with his parents, laughed and said, "You give them my love." Percy said, "Well you give my love to your parents," but Manuel informed him sadly that he was an orphan. "It was nice meeting, you," Percy said, finishing his tea, "but my train at Victoria awaits." Much to his surprise, Manuel insisted on writing a telephone number, telling Percy to contact him next time he was in London. Percy said he would, knowing full well he wouldn't, but pocketed it anyway as a souvenir of an extremely brief and somewhat circumscribed encounter.

Back at the flat he had intended to pack quickly and drive as soon as possible, but concluded he were best to start on Friday, the following morning, at first light, as Julius Caesar invariably did. He would need a clear head, a requirement which contra-indicated socialising with the Townsends that evening, who would never let you refuse a drink. Matters slightly sorted themselves out when Mrs Townsend knocked at the door. She had a small gift for him, and regretted that they were out that evening, but if he could drop her at the hairdressers for her midday appointment, he would save her life. He did it gladly, and then commenced clearing up and packing. Unlike Jet he had no leather suitcase full of tablecloths. One was canvas, the other, compressed cardboard. There had been an ancient trunk which journeyed between Truro and the King's School, and between Truro and Brasenose, but that had been requisitioned by his brother. His possessions and books had expanded somewhat during his first term at Hurstwood. He dithered, wondering how much to take to Truro and bring back, or how much to leave in the flat, and how much he could transport in the car loose, to save acquiring another suitcase or cardboard box. It then seemed a good idea to phone Elizabeth from the call box and afterwards see if he could get a box from the supermarket next to it. But coming out of the flat, he met Mr Townsend, who enquired as to his immediate pursuit, and volunteered the loan of a suitcase and use of his phone. Following the conclusion of his call, he was administered a large glass of sherry, and sat listening to the great man's reminiscences, until Mrs Townsend's return by taxi from the hairdresser's. Mr Townsend quickly hid the sherry glasses on hearing the door go, and motioned Percy to leave with suitcase. Mrs Townsend was effusive and probably accustomed to pretend not to notice the smell of alcohol on her husband's breath.

Early the following morning Percy woke in an anxious frenzy about his car. His father had always impressed on him that motor cars were, for the most part, badly made from faulty components, and garages, dishonest, incompetent or both. Unless you were prepared to spend all your time tinkering under the bonnet, assuming aptitude, knowledge, competence, experience, interest and a decent tool kit, second-hand cars were a nightmare; and new cars were only worth buying with tax relief. The GP practice bought new cars every three years, though Spenser senior thought wistfully of the running boards and leather seats of his childhood. God must have been speaking to Percy in a dream, for looking out of the window he spotted a flat tyre, and when he turned the engine over, it wouldn't start. He had been relying on the Morris to get him to Truro and back via Bath.

Should he get the car sorted or take the train? If he were to take the train, he needed to scale down his luggage. Mr Townsend, who was an early riser, even after a rare evening out, had been looking out of the window under the dim light of the street lamp.

"Trouble at mill, lad," he said as he came out in a heavy red dressing-gown. He was all in favour of the train. He feared break down on the Salisbury Plain. Fortunately, this wasn't the prelude to one of his army stories. "Fancy a spot of breakfast." Percy was tempted, but declined on the grounds there wasn't time. "I must hot foot it to Paddington."

He washed and dressed like lightning, swiftly jettisoned most of his luggage, and was soon out of the flat huffing and puffing to the bus stop. One hour and forty minutes later he was on the train at Paddington with Guardian and sandwich. The single fare was punitively expensive, and used up much of Percy's cash. If only he hadn't made those trips to London. He would still have to fund his fare back to Townsend Towers via Bath, and get the car fixed. His salary was due at the end of the month, but would need to go a long way. He should have cancelled the trip to Bath and bought a return ticket. Then again there were those wonderful coaches he had been brought up to despise, but might save a few shillings. He fell asleep, waking up when coffee was brought round. He managed to complete both cryptic and quick crosswords, feeling pleased with himself.

There was quite a long time between finishing the crosswords and reaching Truro, during which he talked to no-one. He got off at Truro, and unequal to carrying his suitcase all the way to the surgery, and unwilling to pay for a taxi, decided to phone his mum, and see if she would collect him. She was a bit grumpy and said he'd have to wait twenty minutes, which he agreed to, feeling slightly tight-fisted. While waiting, another train had pulled in, and their near neighbour, Maisie Neave, got out. Maisie was larger than life. She was about his mother's age, but with orange hair, and always wore raincoats his mother described as "lairy." She freely described the tribulations of her existence, but you had to be careful not to give her too much information, because she would tell everyone your business, or so his mother had always warned him. Percy had always liked her, and as a child had much admired Mr Neave's motorbike and side-car. Their son, Gordon, was some three years younger than Percy, and as a late, and only, child, had always been the apple of his mother's eye, but no longer. She began a litany of complaints. He hadn't worked at school, and failed the eleven-plus. He'd got work in an office somewhere, but wouldn't knuckle down. He'd got involved with art students, given up work, grown his hair long, and always wore some grubby plimsolls he first bought to play tennis. But worst of all, he had taken to buying bits of furniture which were stored in the garage- I think he's getting his own together -and you could hardly get into his room it was so untidy, and all his father ever said was, "leave the boy alone."

"And to think I used to sweep floors for him," she said, finishing her monologue, and suddenly reflecting on how exactly she intended to complete her journey, said, "I'm going to give his nibs a ring. How are you getting home?" It was fortunate at that moment that Mrs Spenser rolled up in the Ford Cortina, the humblest car possible for a doctor's practice. They were quite happy to give Mrs Neave a lift, but careful not to discuss the tax relief on the vehicle, for fear such important details would be made known to the world at large.

It was not till they had dropped off Mrs Neave and were back in doors that Mrs Spenser ventured to discuss her son's first few months of work. The details of Percy's curriculum did not greatly interest her, nor really his accommodation or motor-car problems. Her big concern was whether he'd got a girl-friend. But rather than adopting the strictest moral code, she thought he would be better to pursue the ladies regardless of serious intent. After all, his brother, who had been much more ruthless at mere seduction, had got a girl-friend, whilst Percy hadn't. In vain he pleaded Miss Evans who was expecting him for the New Year.

Percy switched the conversation to his father, who was still doing paper work in the surgery. She told him he was on some committee investigating whether cannabis was addictive or not, and it was smoking cannabis that had in his opinion changed Gordon, though she wasn't convinced. This was an interesting development.

Chapter Thirteen

Father's Committee

Spenser senior, Albert, was regularly forced to defend himself against a charge of alcoholism, brought by his wife, Margaret. Allusion thereto was perhaps inevitable in his explanations on the subject of Indian hemp, which concluded supper. The meal was only referred to as dinner when they had guests and used the heavy, over-sized knives and forks, stored in the sideboard drawers, and not the lightweight ones with the bone handles, found in the kitchen.

"Well, Percy, what better illustration of addiction can there be than that you witness in your staff-room daily? All that hard-earned money up in smoke, and the result is a vile smell, a bad cough, and twenty years off the user's life, as well as wrinkled skin and bad breath. I even have patients with bronchitis from other people's smoke. After hundreds of years, there is little genetic immunity to tobacco. Unless you really dislike your first cigarette, you need great strength of will not to succumb to addiction, and even more to give them up.

"At least most users of alcohol don't depend on it to get out of bed in the morning and stop their hands shaking, can wait till the sun has gone over the proverbial yard arm before their first snifter, and don't drink till they pass out. Those we dub the drunks and dipsomaniacs are genetically disposed to alcoholism. But that can amount to whole nations. How many North American Indians were cynically introduced to whisky? There are parts of Australia today where alcohol is banned. This is to protect the aboriginal. In cities bars are open from 6.30 to 7.00 of an evening only. That is to protect the white Australian.

"Morphine, heroin and are drugs of clinical dependency as are barbiturates and amphetamine. Users of the latter typically require pills to wake up and pills to sleep.

"Indian hemp, or cannabis, has always been out on a limb, because it isn't instantly addictive, but that only blinds the user to the dangers of its consumption and encourages them. The drug is a stupefacient which seems to deliver a near religious experience and revelation of inner truth. The user becomes hooked on the illusion. The drug stays in the system for a long time, and users can hardly stop themselves going into trances or having paranoid delusions. Thereafter, some users require the drug to stop anxiety and keep from going into a trance, whilst others find it no longer gives them an inner spiritual glow, but gives a bad experience. They see the light and stop.

"Think about *The Strange Tale of Dr Jekyll and Mr Hyde*. At first the doctor takes the pill to become Mr Hyde temporarily. After a while he needs the pill to revert to being Dr Jekyll.

"My guess is that our friend, Gordon, has been smoking with the local art students. Whether it has triggered schizophrenia I don't know, but consumption with the right company will encourage him in his delusion that he has found an alternative reality which doesn't involve going out to work. Maybe it is merely a bourgeois notion that salvation can only be achieved through work, and Gordon is right to eschew humble employment; but I suspect all his art student friends will soon be earning a fortune in graphic design, smoking only Benson and Hedges Special Gold King Size, which are quite addictive enough.

"Unfortunately, the other members of my committee are naïve, and refuse to see the drug is addictive at all. Rather they view its insidious nature as, by its very harmlessness, luring the user into trying other substances, an argument I find tendentious."

He was about to be very rude about his colleagues, using unprofessional language, but Margaret weighed in. What evidence did Albert have about art students or anyone else smoking hemp? Mrs Neave was to blame for spoiling the boy and not pushing him harder at school, and then she turned on her husband, "You go out to the pub very regularly, and come back stinking of tobacco, for all your disapproval of it. You sup a few pints to see the world through rose-tinted spectacles, failing to discern your companions are not warm and wonderful good blokes and diamond geezers, but boring, narrow-minded, blinkered, inadequate wimps, who can't bear the company of their wives."

Albert Spenser took this as a challenge. Rising from the table he enjoined his son, Percy, to join him for a pint. "We'll do the drying up when we come back, Margaret," he added as a sop, thinking the offer might do in place of flowers. He knew very well his wife was a compulsive television viewer, and couldn't wait to have her feet up in front of the box.

Caught in the politics of his parents' marriage, and fearing a heavy session, and the possibility of having to buy an expensive round, Percy volunteered to clear the dishes, and do both washing up and drying up, before accompanying his father or joining him. His father agreed they would go to the pub together after the chores, but had no intention of helping. He picked up a forlorn- looking newspaper, discovering with great joy its crosswords had not been attempted, sat down and nodded off. Thus, Spenser senior and junior reached the pub nearer last orders than opening time. Even so, they each consumed three pints. Percy was never quite sure what his father's friends did, as all talk of shop was barred. Greek and Latin were off limits, as were leather bars, but digs, motor cars and girl-friends weren't. Eventually, the story of a tyrannical schoolmaster who was thereby refused admission to every golf club proved a winner. It was getting a little frosty by the time they left, and Albert seemed less steady on his feet than he should have been. Perhaps like the North American Indians he'd had a little fire water when no-one was looking, and some of Margaret's reservations were not without justification.

Had Albert Spenser paid too much for the practice? Probably, but a substantial amount had been released from the sale of most of the garden to a local builder. This had funded the twins' expensive education. The house, constructed in the Edwardian era, was less than ideal. Occupying a separate wing, the surgery, waiting room, office and downstairs toilet were too small. They harked back to an era when the doctor visited his fee-paying patients, whilst those on the panel waited in the rain.

Entering the main part of the house, the kitchen was a tiny galley, designed for the incarceration of a serf, let out purely to wait on table, and that only on good behaviour. Mrs Spenser objected to fulfilling that role. Sitting and dining rooms both deserved the accolade "reception," though guests and visitors were seldom received. The study had been taken over by Margaret as an overspill office. Albert had adopted the fourth bedroom upstairs as his study, but had at some stage started to sleep in there, on abandoning the matrimonial bed, whilst maintaining shares in the matrimonial wardrobe. The boys had initially shared a bedroom, but later had their own, despite so much time spent away at school. Albert had long been minded to requisition one of their rooms for sleeping purposes, but all that seemed to be under his wife's control. In any event, he liked sleeping in the study, which was quiet and received the morning sun, but not before seven. Furthermore, if ever he was "studying," he headed for whichever reception room he fancied. He was thus a man who could never find anything, and would charge around the house swearing, in the vain belief that inappropriate language would assist his search. This was always an excuse for Margaret to sulk, an activity or non-activity she was very good at, though a casual observer might have thought she sulked for too long, quite unnecessarily, and quite counter-productively.

Percy took his time getting to sleep. A longer stroll would have been better that evening, and half the quantity of beer. However, on a winter's night, without a dog to exercise, anybody walking further than there and back to the nearest pub would have been viewed with the utmost suspicion. His head was in a spin, contemplating the truth that, far from a welcome retreat from his life at Hurstwood Grammar, he was in the front row of a far deadlier combat. How much better or worse would it be when and if his brother arrived, with or without girlfriend? When he woke, he couldn't decide whether it would be better to keep out of everybody's way as their working day started, although it was a Saturday, or if having a lie in would be seen as lazy and disloyal. Sometimes his mother had domestic help and sufficient assistance in the surgery, and sometimes did everything herself. First things first. He took a shower and came down wearing an old dressing gown that had been hanging on the back of the bedroom door, the provenance of which eluded him. The dining room table had been cleared, and Percy crept guiltily into the kitchen. His mother might have been waiting with an axe to judge by the venom with which she said, "Do you know what the time is?" It was ten-past-nine. Not perhaps being up to the role of Clytemnestra so early in the day, she dismounted from her high horse to ask Percy in a more measured tone what he'd like for breakfast. Percy forbore the temptation to set her off by saying, "Oh, is there a choice?" and put in a humble petition for a boiled egg. At some stage the rather dysfunctional serving hatch had been replaced by a Formica-topped breakfast bar with wobbly stools. Percy sat here whilst his mother rehearsed her grievances.

Had, of course, she not married Dr Spenser, or "your father" when feeling particularly venomous, she would at the very least have been a ballerina, actress or M.P. That was a familiar complaint which normally went in one ear and out the other, rather like his great uncle's first world war stories. There was a difference. He tried to follow his uncle's accounts, but somehow always lost the plot, with the guilty feeling this was all first-hand history which should be kept for posterity; but he was all too well aware of every twist in his mother's lamentation. From

87

childhood he could dimly remember his mother telling stories about a magic snail called Sidney which lived in the garden and had gold wallpaper inside his shell. If only she had confined her talents to the adventures of Sidney!

But even though she had married dear Albert, she might have had more time to play golf, tennis and bridge, if he hadn't been so downright disorganised, so "scatty" as she put it, taking no interest in the running of his practice, but rather falling out with his patients when he wouldn't prescribe sleeping pills or tranquillisers, insisting they should form encounter groups, which he had no intention of organising or running, because all he ever wanted to do was get to the pub as soon as possible of an evening, and Percy was to watch out for the "secret shorts" as she put it, an expression Percy thought would have gone down well with Jet.

Percy offered to play golf with his mother, if there were some spare clubs available, weather and time permitting, but wasn't sure she was really interested. "Don't think marriage is a bed of roses, Percy. You're an incurable romantic and far too sensitive."

If a man's best friend should be his wife, a boy's best friend ought to be his mother; but Percy's mother had her own agenda, driven by every one of her life's little adventures, and could not or would not take any interest in Percy's career at Hurstwood, his lodgings, his motor car or his uncertain feelings for Miss Evans. He was on his own. She was soon on to the follies of his brother, and not above contradicting what she might have said earlier. Whether he was right or wrong to be living so flagrantly over the brush, and who was taking advantage of whom she wasn't sure, but it would all end in tears, and his job had no security. She lay awake at night worrying about it.

Percy was about to upset the apple cart entirely with the devastating line "Can I go now?" when she came to a natural conclusion. She was going to do a spell in the office, would Percy tidy the kitchen, make some sandwiches for lunch and come shopping with her that afternoon. By this stage he would have agreed to anything, and thought he had got off rather lightly. He said "Yes," and gave one of his irresistible smiles.

There was always a degree of contradiction in his mother's views. On the one hand, his brother was right to be a ruthless seducer, because ruthless seducers always settled down with one of their conquests. On the other hand, relationships might fall apart at any moment, and the ruthless seducer was more likely to end up in the lurch. Did women all crave happy marriages, he mused, or could they all be seduced by fair means or foul and against their better judgment? Should he have pulled Miss Evan's knickers down and had her on the back seat of the Morris on their first date? Why hadn't he? Should he cancel the trip to Bath? He decided to finish the chores, get dressed and go for a walk.

That afternoon, assisting his mother with not quite the last of the Christmas shopping, he rather admired the shop girls, and was a little aghast on the way home when his mother said she'd seen him eye the girls up, but he shouldn't get involved with a girl who was beneath him.

"Chance would be a fine thing," Percy thought to himself, but then recalling the many different ways the disciples of Socrates agreed with his spurious arguments without using the word "yes," said, "how right you are, Mother, how very true!" She was slightly taken aback, and said nothing more on the short drive home.

It had to be admitted the Spenser household was heavily dependent on Mrs Spenser's cooking, which was of the meat and two veg variety, and therefore Percy found himself in the narrow galley peeling spuds. His mother had remembered his interest in botany, and asked if he had been pursuing it. Percy had to say he hadn't, guiltily remembering botany was his original connection with Jet, and there had actually been times when they had researched the wild meadow flowers of Oxford.

89

Margaret then advised there would be a cocktail party Thursday the 23rd December, and somebody's daughter who might be there might be interested in flowers at least, if not the ancient Greeks, classical drama or Ovid's *Art of Love*. Percy wasn't sure what his mother knew of this work, which he himself had not studied, and suggested they should wait and see; but added he hoped it wasn't formal dress.

"Good heavens, no. The usual moth-eaten sports jackets I should imagine with leather patches on the sleeves." Percy thought of Mr Townsend and smiled to himself, but his mother had spotted it.

"What are you grinning about?"

He commenced an account of Mr Townsend, knowing full well his mother's interest would be strictly limited, and she was likely to interrupt to ask him for his views on the economic outlook or anything else that came into her head. She was most intrigued by the fact that neither Mr nor Mrs Townsend drove, despite not being short of a bob or two, and didn't have a television.

"You meet some funny people," she said, and then told him to seek out his father and find out if he were secretly imbibing. Percy was glad to escape the kitchen, but not enthralled by the idea of covert observations.

His father was sitting in the lounge reading *The Lancet*.

"The sun's over the yard arm," he said. "Drop of whisky, not a word to the trouble and strife." He poured Percy a modest measure, and then said, "Do you need any money? You've got that silly car to run." Percy was thus bribed to keep quiet.

Albert Spenser had a low opinion of the medical profession. Nobody knew what they were talking about, there were absurd hierarchies of respect, restrictive practices and inbuilt inefficiencies were legion, and patients were their own worst enemies. Half the people who came to his surgery deserved to be sent away with a flea in their ear. The other half would have got better without his intervention. "I have often thought of ending it all with a bare bodkin," he suddenly said in a thespian manner. "Or rather the doctor does in the play I'm never going to write, but would run and run in the West End, if ever I did."

Percy understood his father totally at this point, and knew exactly why he needed to sup ale and come out with all this, just as his mother came out with her speeches without the help of stimulants at all.

Percy asked about the prospective cocktail party, in case he could get any better information, but none was forthcoming. His father returned to *The Lancet*, and Percy went off to read some more of the detestable Bury's *History of Greece*.

By the time it came to dinner, the whisky had worn off, and Percy did rather think a glass of red wine wouldn't have gone amiss, but stuck to Malvern water. He offered to do the washing up, and suggested he didn't want to go to the pub. His father wasn't at all put out, being quite capable of going there by himself. His mother probably thought it a good result, as she could get to the television quicker, and would know where Percy was when she fancied bending his ear.

Chapter Fourteen

The Cocktail Party

Truro society was much like anywhere else. The doctors, solicitors, accountants, bank managers and other professional men may have fancied they wafted about in clouds of glory, but neither they nor the local landowners could afford or were willing to throw a decent party. That great service to the drinking classes was performed by a shady elite of businessmen, dressed in flashy suits, with kipper ties, or in leather jackets with a gold medallion round their open neck. Belying the equation of wealth with being well-heeled, they often wore suede shoes, which didn't need polishing and never looked respectable. They drove Jaguars by preference, having traded up their Zephyrs, were frequently divorced, and homed in on golf clubs, always seen to be the key to upward mobility for those with no old school tie. They knew their manners well enough to buy the crusty colonels a large drink, who hovered so expectantly by the bar, and knew a good chap when they saw one.

New and old money thus met as it always has done, but when the self-made man looked to his children's education, always a priority, he wasn't so stupid as to pass up on the eleven-plus. If they got to the grammar school, there was no nonsense about the fee-paying school with the charitable status, designated "public," unlike the golf club which was "private," but members only. They only went to a fee-paying school if they failed the eleven plus, which usually meant they also failed the entrance test to the "public" school anyway. There were fourth-division private schools, and religious foundations, distinguished by their colourful uniforms, to which the children went and left with one O-level, but all the right connections.

The Spensers were well-placed to add their imprimatur of respectability to arrivistes, and had thus been invited to the Sheridans' pre-Christmas party. They were new to Truro, but had already made their mark, buying a house with a tennis court, pond and all the reception rooms you could possibly want. Albert had accepted the invitation quite eagerly, always being anxious to view his richer patients in their natural habitat. Margaret was less keen, feeling the lack of a new dress, mink stole, and real, as opposed to costume, jewellery. With her corns she couldn't manage high-heels, but always felt a fool in Clarks casuals, despite the leeway granted to doctors' wives in the wearing of orthopedic footwear. Percy thought there might be some girls there, despite being due to attend on Miss Elizabeth Evans for the new year. He had chatted briefly with her on the phone, and learnt that her father's aunt on his mother's side, aunty Wynnie, had come to stay for Christmas. She was occupying the room designated for Percy's use, and Percy's visit was thus dependent on her going home as soon as possible. She wasn't in the habit of staying too long, being petrified of coming home to burst pipes, which was fortunate, because Mrs Evans soon tired of her eccentric relation by marriage. Aunty Wynnie had always eschewed housework, and invariably travelled in an old coat the dog used to sleep on, and shamefully worn-out shoes, without socks or stockings. She was a bit of an embarrassment, but made people laugh.

It was slightly too far to walk, but Margaret had volunteered to stay sober. In any event, Albert had great confidence in his drunk driving skills. It was a short distance and unlikely to be icy. Percy recalled his nightmarish drive after his afternoon encounter with Josephine Tourtel, surprised at the complaisance of Mr Townsend, who had the utmost faith in any driver, perhaps a necessary requirement for someone who had never even mastered riding a bicycle.

Percy really wished he had a decent wardrobe of clothing. However well he looked after his Prince of Wales check suit, it was his only suit. He had one pair of grey flannel trousers, a battered sports jacket, one pair of jeans and a bag full of old and colourful woolly jumpers. They were all right for wearing round the house, but that was all. Margaret suggested the obvious that his twin brother might have something stored away, especially as he either had more money than Percy to spend on clothes in the first place, or else spent a higher percentage of it on clothes, if the same or less. Albert and Margaret had long considered it remarkable just how smart Percy could look, when he spent so little. William's drawers proved to contain some mod shirts, and hanging in his cupboard was a velvet jacket. "Just the ticket," as Albert said.

Albert's best suit, the only one that wasn't worn to a shine, was a heavy tweed, better suited to outdoor life in the dales than an over-heated lounge. He was tempted to requisition the velvet jacket, but thought better of it. Margaret suggested he wore some ghastly cardigan she had bought him one Christmas, and he readily agreed. He thought he owed it her, having worn it on rather too few occasions to proclaim his admiration for the gift and the giver. The party was the ideal opportunity.

That didn't solve Margaret's dilemma. To her mind the King's School Canterbury had been funded out of her dress allowance. "I've nothing to wear, thanks to you," she screamed at Albert, who was about to say, "But you've got your red, white or blue, skirt or dress," when he couldn't for the life of him identify any of her clothes whatsoever. He might as well be asked what the Queen wore at her summer garden party. "I'd be ashamed to go to a parish social in any of my outfits," she said witheringly, not that she ever did or ever had, but it seemed like a good line to use. There was, of course, something that would do, there aways was, and who was she trying to impress anyway?

They all looked quite presentable when they arrived at the party, after parking some distance away down the road. Fortunately, it wasn't raining and Margaret wasn't wobbling on stiletto heels. Not knowing at what point being late ceased to be fashionable, but became rude, they had intended to come on the dot, which might be a good excuse to leave

94

early. However, William had phoned to say he wasn't coming for Christmas, but might, only might, for the New Year. This had set Margaret off. She burst into tears at the ingratitude of it all, and then had to re-do her make-up.

They were disarmed by the welcome. Guests had arrived unfashionably early, and the party was in full swing. Their hosts had hired a butler to take coats and waiters to offer champagne or punch. Their bottle of gin was received graciously, with "You really shouldn't have!" before their hosts disappeared. They looked round to see who they knew, spotting only those familiar faces belonging to people you know you know from somewhere, but can't quite recall. It was impossible not to refuse a generous glass of punch of uncertain strength, and Albert, being naturally sociable, got swept up with a crowd of people he didn't know; but at least it got him away from Margaret. Percy was left holding the baby, a baby which found the unwonted punch rather agreeable. The waiter was rather handsome and not averse to flirting with an older woman in the course of duty, with the sinister intent of helping her lose her inhibitions over a second and third glass of punch.

"I'm going to find your father and box his ears," she said rather feistily, the mixture of spirits, fruit juice, perry and vermouth, having rather gone to her head, lurching off in her Clarks Casuals, cream blouse and the kilt she had found at the back of the wardrobe. Percy watched her go and noticed a young lady with goofy teeth. She seemed the more attractive or more approachable for that reason, and they were soon having an intellectual conversation of a kind which had eluded Percy at Oxford. But after a while it took a turn for the worse. Felicity Sheridan was at Sussex University doing a course in philosophy, sociology and psychology. This was a little off Percy's radar. He had studied the Greek philosophers, but was mindful of two definitions of philosophy, one, that all learning and enquiry started off as philosophy, but usually turned into something else, and philosophy was what was left over; the second, that philosophy was what philosophers happened to be arguing about at the time. After the Ionians and Plato, he had done a little bit on the early Christian fathers, which he had kept secret from Mr Townsend; but knew nothing of the modern world. Felicity, on the other hand, had several modern bibles, *The Divided Self* by R D Laing, *The Constitution of Liberty* by Friedrich Hayek and *The Critique of Dialectical Reason* by Jean Paul Sartre. She was a very earnest young lady, and didn't quite appreciate it when Percy said "It's all Greek to me." Percy was becoming bolder as his glass was stealthily refilled. He had an overwhelming desire to escort the young lady upstairs and smack her bottom. Would that sort out her divided self? Perhaps she had read his mind or was as inebriated as him. With a gushing unsteadiness she suggested he came upstairs to look at her books. Out of the corner of his eye, he could see his mother dressed in someone's fake ocelot fur coat, someone else's Russian-style hat and smoking a cigarette in a long holder.

Felicity's bedroom was at the back of the house, overlooking the pond. How much pretence was there to her books? They were soon snogging on the bed, but she was at pains to stress that it was not to go any further. Whether it would have gone any further is a moot point, because suddenly there were loud screams from the garden, "Oh my God, she's fallen in." In all the excitement Percy hadn't taken his shoes off, and was able to sprint down the stairs and through the lounge into the garden. The pond was not deep, and his mother had not hurt herself, but was sobering up even as she sat in the cold, dirty water. The nice wine waiter was the one to help her out. Albert had passed out in the bushes. Mrs Sheridan thought the whole thing very funny, and escorted a dripping Margaret to the upstairs bathroom. Percy thought he should at least attend to his father, rather amused at the idea he couldn't take his parents anywhere. A rather angry woman with a red face approached Percy as he was trying to revive his father, "He put his hand down my bosom." Percy could see what a temptation the dress was, but felt the need to placate her.

"I'm very sorry, you see my father is not used to drinking, and the punch must have gone to his head. I'll drive him home, and he won't bother you again."

"Tell him to keep his hands to himself."

"Most certainly."

People did seem to be awfully drunk, and Percy couldn't help feeling that hardly anyone had noticed his parents disgracing themselves, and certainly nobody cared. Felicity had re-appeared and helped make a cup of tea for Albert.

"God, what a cleavage," was all he could say, before he started hyper-ventilating. Percy wasn't aware his father was prone to do this, but had an idea you should ask the patient to breathe in and out of a paper bag. Felicity was dispatched to find one, but by the time she had, Albert's breathing had slowed down a bit. So he did nothing, but felt bad for not ringing 999 to get an ambulance.

By then, guests were heading to the supper room, as his mother came down stairs in Mrs Sheridan's gardening clothes, a tartan check blouse, some ill-fitting slacks and some rope-soled deck shoes. Margaret said she would sit with her husband, and Percy and Felicity could go into supper.

The spread was as magnificent as cold salad dishes with every conceivable meat could be. Percy and Felicity sat arguing about everything as Felicity was both shrill and feisty, quite unsuitable for a long-term relationship. Percy was never very forceful, but was certainly no push-over. There was some ginger beer on the table, which went rather well with the salad. They eventually held hands and stepped back out into the garden. Albert had recovered and was back inside sitting with Margaret on the settee, and talking to the lady in the red dress, who had calmed down, and now appeared to be flirting with Albert.

Felicity was becoming amorous. "Oh Percy, you make the Greeks so interesting; you must be a very good teacher." They kissed discreetly in the darkest part of the garden, but Percy suddenly stared to worry that she was the clinging type, and he shouldn't get involved, when she burst into tears. What was the matter?

"You can't possibly understand," she said, "Just leave me alone." With that she ran off, leaving Percy mystified. Perhaps it was time to round up his parents and suggest they left. They were inside where he had left them, but the woman in the red dress had gone.

"Do you think we should go?" he propositioned his parents. "I'm sure you don't want to stay for the dancing." He forbore to say, "Haven't you disgraced yourselves enough?"

Margaret took a different view. "Percy, you're such a spoil sport. Find that girl and make a man of yourself. I'm going to circulate."

At that she rose and went off to find someone more interesting to talk to than her husband or son. Tom Jones was singing "What's New Pussycat?" Margaret felt she was a re-born pussycat. She was soon swept up into the dancing. Percy could see his mother was "making out" and felt obliged to get involved in some boys' conversation with his father. Albert probably thought the same, but neither of them could think of anything to say. Albert eventually broke the silence.

"It really was love at first sight when I met your mother. She was in one of her sitting-in-a-pond moments of drunkenness in a borrowed and garish item. We both knew party tricks were best kept for occasional use, and avoided the joint consumption of alcohol in our courtship and marriage. I know I go to the pub and enjoy a snifter when the sun's gone over the yard-arm, but it's the company I need. Your mother doesn't need my company. She's quite happy with the telly and her bridge friends. I don't personally much care for her bridge friends or the telly. I suppose I'm a secret misogynist. Now, what's going on with you and that young lady?"

"I don't know. She keeps changing her mind, but I'm not sure what about."

"Well, keep a low profile. We don't want to upset the Sheridans. Not that they're private patients. No one is these days. You don't want to rush into marriage, but you don't want to stay single all your life."

Albert paused for a moment, feeling in his intoxication he had said something terribly profound, but then seemed to change his mind about Felicity. "I'd grab that Felicity, if I were you. I'm sure she's a bit of a goer."

Percy didn't know whether to be amused or shocked by his father's candour. Someone seemed to have turned up the volume on the radiogram, as "Tired of Waiting for You" by the Kinks blasted out. Was Felicity tired of waiting?

They both wandered into the lounge. Margaret decided she would grab her husband and make him dance, as if to demonstrate to the woman in the red dress that any interest shown by her husband was of a transient nature. She was, however, flirting with an elderly gentleman in a dinner jacket, who appeared mesmerised by her cleavage, and refraining with difficulty from committing what would undoubtedly have been the second indecent assault upon her person.

Felicity then floated in, and by that time seemed to have calmed down. Percy started dancing with her. The Beach Boys were now singing "California Girls." Perhaps life was easier in California, perhaps Percy should abandon himself to a predatory promiscuity, and give up his Sunday School morality and yearning for suburban respectability.

Having danced with Felicity for a bit, he decided he couldn't stand her, even as a friend, but then felt bad about it, as if he had given her the booby prize in a beauty competition. Fortunately, someone else grabbed her at that point, and Percy found himself chatting to Sheridan and some of his business friends. They were amazed by the idea of him teaching Latin and Greek. He could never earn decent money doing that. However, none of them actually offered him a job, and though they admitted the holidays were good, the merits of the contributory pension scheme were not discussed. Then someone commenced a long and rather boring dirty joke. Percy could dimly recall someone from the King's School Christian Union telling him he should turn to Christ and not keep listening to the same dirty jokes. He had replied he'd like to listen to some new ones. That seemed to sum the situation up, and the teller turned his attention to the Irish.

Percy walked off to refill his glass, and then thought it would be nice to eat some more. Back in the dining room the elderly gentleman was filling the plate of the lady in the red dress. He joined them, and engaged in small talk. The woman was soon immersed in Percy's exaggerated account of Mr and Mrs Townsend, the Greenline bus and old Mr Ridley. He made the classics department of Hurstwood Grammar a great deal more interesting than it could possibly be in anyone's wildest imagination, so much so he could hardly wait to be back.

The party came to an end. The Spensers said goodbye, Margaret clutching a shopping bag containing her wet clothes, and promising to return the borrowed items, and pay for the cleaning of the fake ocelot coat. Mrs Sheridan wasn't a bit bothered about the coat, thinking Margaret's adventures in the pond quite the most amusing spectacle she had seen for ages. The Spensers could definitely come again, though they'd probably be too embarrassed. Having sobered up, Albert drove the short distance home confidently, without being too reckless; and on their return indoors, refused any discussion on the party.

After her exhibition in the pond, Margaret recovered more of her sense of humour, and was reluctant to put on her performance as put-upon-martyr. It was Christmas in any event, even if William wasn't there. There was far too much cold turkey. Presents were rather modest. Percy hadn't spent very much on the offering he had given his parents. It was perhaps good that they hadn't wasted too much on something unsuitable, but even so the handkerchiefs and socks were a bit tight-fisted, or so he thought rather ungratefully. His father had after all lent him some money. Then there came a bomb-shell, which paradoxically disappointed Percy, but simplified matters. Elizabeth phoned to say Aunty Wynnie had had a slight stroke. Nothing much wrong with her, but she couldn't talk. She was dumb-struck. This was arguably a great blessing for those who might otherwise have to listen to her; but she couldn't really go back to her filthy bungalow in Weston-super-Mare, or not for a while. And really, they would have to tackle the thirty-year backlog in housework to ensure on her return that neighbours, the social services, relations etc would be better able to help her, and she would be better able to help herself. Percy couldn't come for the New Year, but Elizabeth would happily see him again when they were back at school. Indeed, she sounded very loving over the phone, and Percy responded with great longing. However, it would reduce his expenditure. He planned to return on the coach. Meanwhile Mr Townsend had come up trumps, arranging for the car to be fixed. Percy could settle the bill out of his December salary.

Chapter Fifteen

An Inn of Court

Percy decided not to stay in Truro for the New Year. He didn't want to get caught in any cross-fire if his brother came with girl-friend; but did rather regret the long Thursday coach ride back to London, vowing never to do it again. It was quite late by the time he got back, but the Townsends were still up. They invited him in and presented him with a bumper of something which went to his head quite rapidly. He regaled them with the account of his mother falling in the pond, and they were most amused. It was a good story, and all the better for being true.

Percy got on with his ancient history notes and set books, and greatly looked forward to next meeting Elizabeth. The Townsends kept asking him in to help finish eating the vast amounts of food prepared for the festive season and lessen the guilt of their otherwise unsocial drinking habits, mainly Mr Townsend's.

Percy managed to re-unite with Elizabeth before term started. She was still playing hard to get, but that seemed a good indicator. She didn't appear to lack passion. However, there were a lot of other matters on his mind when term started. With the arrival of Mr Sweet to complete the complement of English teachers, and the partial retirement of Mrs Thompson, there were changes to the timetables. Mr Tourtel was restored to teach more Latin and less English, but not to teach any Greek. Mr Rowntree flexed his muscles as head of the department.

There in the first year was the rather timid and diminutive Metcalfe, who seemed on the perpetual verge of tears, especially after Mr Rowntree's regular grillings. The boy's mental state had been delicately raised with Mr Rowntree by more than one of his colleagues, but his attitude was that his teaching methods, though robust, were successful, and he could hardly make allowance for character weakness. He thought it toughened a pupil to be exposed to a style that might prepare him for army discipline. He also quoted the verse from the Bible, "Let him who is without sin cast the first stone." There was a certain amount of ear-tweaking and cuffing of the back of the neck, as well as the occasional slap round the head. Captain Turpin's predecessor had thrashed boys quite unmercifully in his time, but sympathetic pals on the bench had secured his acquittal on more than one summons. Mr Rowntree had never laid a finger on any boy. What he did was to point a ruler in a boy's face when asking them for parts of verbs and nouns, and would beat time with the ruler pending their reply. He would put them through hell, and make them write lines should they give the wrong answer. It was unfortunate that Metcalfe's father was a distinguished QC. The charge for which Mr Rowntree was summoned to the magistrate's court was assault, by the pointing of a ruler in Metcalfe junior's face.

There was somewhat of a furore. There had been no prior representations to either the headmaster or Mr Rowntree himself, but there were whispers some sixth-formers were prepared to attest to their own experiences at Mr Rowntree's hand. Metcalfe junior was as terrified as ever, caught between father and teacher.

Captain Turpin attempted to persuade Metcalfe QC to drop the action, and received an invitation to attend Metcalfe's chambers with Mr Rowntree. One January morning they met at the station, went to Charing Cross and took the underground to the Temple. Neither of them had ever been to an Inn of Court before. This was a different world, one where the unguarded might easily be cowed by an impressive mixture of power and politeness. "What exactly did they object to? Had they engaged a solicitor to speak at the hearing?" They were made to feel in the wrong for having dared to come the chambers at all, even more for being offered a rather superior brand of cigarette.

"Listen to me, will you," said the captain. "Mr Rowntree is a highly competent, efficient and fair teacher. He does not assault his pupils.

My staff are well aware that boys are not to be assaulted. If there is to be any corporal punishment, it would be recorded and administered by myself. I am pleased to say there hasn't been any."

Metcalfe QC smiled and peered over the top of his spectacles. His desk was piled up with briefs, neatly tied in pink; the glass fronted bookcases at his rear reflected the winter sun. "You fail to distinguish between an assault and a battery. Such a failing is common among laymen. When you point a ruler in someone's face, there is an implied threat that you will hit them with it. That is the assault. If you do hit them with it, that is the battery. Mr Rowntree has not been charged with assault and battery. He has only been charged with assault. You might think that a school teacher is entitled to rely on a legal presumption that in the exercise of his office he may overrule the strict application of the common law, a privilege denied to the ordinary person when addressing, say, a shop assistant or bus conductor. That matter can initially be determined by a magistrate. However, an appeal will be available by way of case stated to the Queen's Bench Division of the High Court, if there is no dispute as to the facts. I take it there is no denial that a ruler was pointed in my son's face. The dispute relates only to whether it was an assault, and if an assault, whether it was in some way justified. You may rest assured I take a keen interest in my son's scholastic progress in Latin and other subjects. I am convinced that Grammar schools can and do deliver as good an education as boys would get at the best public schools. I went to one of the best public schools, and remain aghast at the terror that was inflicted on me there. I don't want to see my son suffer the same way. He is a sensitive lad. Will that be all?"

"I think you're taking a very narrow view of the law," said Captain Turpin. "The magistrates may well find Mr Rowntree not guilty. The success of your subsequent appeal would be uncertain. Of course, we would sooner you dropped the charges, and were you to do that, we might review our teaching methods."

"Exactly how?" interjected Mr Rowntree, feeling alarmed.

"You could maybe adopt a friendlier tone. Make a game out of it."

"Learning Latin is not a game, but if you really insist, I will agree not to point rulers in faces."

"It just so happens," replied Sir William Metcalfe QC with the ghost of a smile on his face, "that an undertaking has been prepared for your signature. It lists the kind of behaviours we consider are intimidating and may amount to an assault. I also consider the excessive imposition of lines should be proscribed for failing to construe, parse or otherwise identify parts of verbs or nouns, without prejudice to the normal imposition of homework." He produced copies for both Captain Turpin and Mr Rowntree to sign and retain, and a third for his own records. "Would you like to consider the undertaking over coffee?"

A pot of coffee was brought in at that very moment of a quality far exceeding anything the captain or Mr Rowntree had ever drunk before. There was also a most impressive selection of biscuits. "I will leave you to your deliberations," the QC said, vacating his desk, "and feel free to smoke another cigarette." He left the box with the lid up and vacated the room. Passing Clouds were a rare treat.

"You better sign it," the captain said. "I'm sure it's not legally binding, and won't serve as any sort of precedent. And we'll put Metcalfe in a different class, without prejudice to the need for boys to be homogeneous." (Education theory demanded grading by end of year exam results to facilitate competition in the marks to be obtained for homework and class room tests on a level playing field. Boys were to be fighting for their form position as if in a boxing ring. That was the supposed spur to academic progress. It ignored the widespread falsification of marks handed in for copied homework or tests completed as the answers were given.) "Do excuse me," he then said, going off in search of the toilet.

It wasn't long before three copies of the document had been signed and witnessed, and the headmaster and classics head emerged from the chambers feeling slightly sheepish. The nearest pub proved an irresistible temptation. "Let me buy you a half," the captain said, leading the way. "Let's imagine we've been called to the bar."

He ordered two halves of best bitter and a double scotch. The whisky went straight to his head and turned defeat into victory. He'd got the better of Metcalfe all right. This would be a story for the next Rotary Club lunch. Mr Rowntree was reflective. The terrorisation of small boys was an instinctive gift and did not depend on the imposition of vicious punishment, however desirable that might have been. He liked to think that older boys who had survived the regime and gone on to study Latin admired him, and appreciated what was only his little joke, even if it weren't part of a game. It was going to need a lot more to knock him off the pedestal on which he had placed himself.

The journey back to school took place in silence. As the whisky wore off, the captain felt humiliated, and all because a wretched snivelling child's father spent sixpence more on every packet of cigarettes, double on every packet of biscuits, and his minions knew how to percolate coffee, a task quite beyond his wife, who had failed miserably at every attempt.

The full truth was never revealed to Percy. Metcalfe junior was moved into a higher class, and a luckless victim from the higher class relegated. "We must all be homogeneous," the headmaster told him when forced to give an explanation by the boy's baffled father.

"We must all look the other way, without getting run over," Mr Tourtel said, whilst Mrs Thompson wore an air of sadness, feeling she had nurtured a viper in her bosom.

Chapter Sixteen

Poetry Workshop

Though small of stature, Hamish Campbell Sweet had rapidly acquired an outsize reputation for near lunacy. He was full of boundless enthusiasm, but always ready to go off on whatever tangent might be offered. He was totally convinced that any boy could write brilliant poetry if only they gave free rein to their opinions and creativity. Not for him a detailed study of rhyme and metre which he disdained, without quite considering what poetic devices lay hidden in free verse formations or what might better be described as a prose poem. One class had been rather shocked when told to write down their feelings on seeing a large spider. Had "Spiders" been set as the weekend essay, no doubt the boys could all have come up with something, but a poem was something else. The results weren't terribly inspiring. One wrote:

My mother's an arachnophobe.
My father thinks she's silly.
She seems to see them everywhere,
Even on his willy.

Another wrote:
You don't amount to much in size,
But spin a deadly trap for flies.
I see you in the kitchen sink
When I go there to have a drink.
You're cute, but have a nasty bite.
To kiss you then would not be right.
This hoover now will suck you up,
And make it safe for our young pup.
Farewell my many-legged friend,
I shed my tears for your sad end.

Hamish was incensed, and in the ensuing lesson nearly gave way to manic rage; but the situation was eased when someone asked if spiders could think like human beings, and could you be a spider in another life? This was a suitable cue to express his Buddhist views, and he was soon lecturing on the sin of treading on ants, because they were human after all. In his next poetry-writing lesson, he turned his attention to the Berlin Wall which had swallowed up the old Brandenburg Gate. This, he thought, was a symbolic site for the re-crucifixion of Jesus. The class were asked to compose a poem for homework, with the promise that he knew of a poetry magazine to which entries might be submitted for publication after consideration by the class. These were the two best entries.

Poem One

Did not Napoleon first use this Gate
For his triumphal entry, when he took
Its quadriga to Paris and his throne?
And overthrown, was that not made anew
With Prussian Iron Cross and oak tree leaves?
And did ambassadors beneath its arch
Not pass to prove their diplomatic rights?
And later when the Nazis came to power,
Was not that quadriga their emblem proud?
And when the Russians marched into Berlin,
Did not that Gate sustain mere bullet holes,
Then stand repaired in hope of better days?
But on that Sunday of barbed wired shame,
Was it not shuttered in a shameful wall,
That cut off West from East? O brave new world!
And was not Jesus Christ re-crucified
Upon that Berlin gate, the Brandenburg?

Poem Two

Not only torn by war, alas,
But torn by a raw, edgy peace,
A peace with wire and watch towers,
A peace with sub-machine guns,
An armed, bristling peace.
War had seemed friendly, comforting,
We could fight, then kiss.
But in the shadow of the Wall,
In the shadow of the bomb,
I doubt we could hold hands,
Even fleetingly.
I doubt we could embrace
Or love.
I see you, Jesus, outlined
There on the Gate,
Cased in concrete.
From your crown of thorns,
Your crown of barbed wire,
The blood seeps down the stone,
Your wooden cross calcifies.
Your light shines briefly in the darkness,
And then the darkness puts it out.

The ambivalent eroticism in the second poem seemed somewhat shocking, but its author explained it as symbolic of love and forgiveness. Mr Sweet wholeheartedly went along with it. However, there were others watching. Mr Duvivier was supportive but cautious, Mr Lunt rather wary about copyrights and sending off poems to outside sources. The only place for publication was the school magazine. Mr Sweet was a little obstinate, and Captain Turpin got involved. He didn't like the second poem at all, and thought both poems had exonerated the Nazis, though rightly deploring the Soviets. Neither could be sent off elsewhere or put in the school magazine. Captain Turpin was the president of the school Christian Union, and had already opposed Mr Sweet's attempt to form a Buddhist society. Mr Sweet was definitely out of luck, as well as out of favour. He had been staying in Percy's former lodgings, and over confident to the point of hubris in his ability to charm the most savage of beasts. For all that he was a natural dog person, the dog bit his hand rather badly. It required medical treatment with stitches. The landlady thought it was all Mr Sweet's fault. Mr Sweet thought it was his karma to blame and wasn't going to report the matter to the police, although the hospital and the school thought he should. Mr Townsend thought it very funny. He suggested Mr Sweet moved into the flat with Percy and slept on the sofa, as long as he didn't roll his disgusting cigarettes with the liquorice papers, or smoke anything in the flat or car. Percy had little choice in the matter and was rather resigned to being a full-time chauffeur to Mr Townsend and Mr Sweet, as well as picking up old Mr Ridley, who certainly didn't get any younger. He was at least able to see Elizabeth at weekends.

Hamish was a decided chatterbox, and though Percy had spent much of his time at Oxford sitting up late listening to self-opinionated conversationalists, he was somewhat out of practice, and had moreover to be up in the morning. Granted, Hamish could be said to have bold ideas, interestingly expressed, but Percy wasn't writing a coded report on him for the benefit of future employers or seats of learning. He was at the receiving end regardless, especially when attempting to write up his Greek history notes. He would start to get a little short-tempered and forceful, retreating to his bedroom, cutting off Hamish in mid flow.

Mr Townsend's brooding, if not actually angry, silence was in evidence most mornings. This bothered Percy not one whit, but he was afraid Hamish might break the unwritten rule and attempt conversation. He needn't have been. Even Hamish could, in his words, pick up the vibes. They were rewarded by being invited to dinner the first Friday evening. It was Mrs Townsend who was fascinated by the whimsical Scot, as he was known, not Mr Townsend. Mr Townsend was seldom fascinated by anything or anyone, and hardly fascinating, except to himself. It wasn't clear whether Hamish was eating out of Mrs Townsend's hands, or the other way round; but when the conversation got round to the fact that Hamish hadn't been sleeping too well on the sofa, she offered him a half-bottle of sleeping pills. Her story was as follows. She had first been prescribed some slimming pills. These gave her boundless energy, but she couldn't sleep, and his Lordship objected to her vacuuming the house at midnight. The doctor then prescribed her some sleeping pills. She took them for a couple of nights, then stopped taking pills altogether, and resigned herself to being fat, and keeping herself as far away from the vacuum cleaner as possible, whatever time it was.

Percy stayed Saturday night at Elizabeth's. Coming back Sunday afternoon, he found Hamish dead to the world on the settee. Some sort of alarm bells rang, and Percy noticed the empty bottle of sleeping pills. He couldn't rouse Hamish, and knocked frantically on the Townsend's door. Mrs Townsend answered the door rather blearily as if she had been enjoying an afternoon nap in the armchair. She responded to Percy's near-hysteria and called for an ambulance. They were surprisingly quick coming and departed with Hamish and the empty bottle. Mrs Townsend felt like a criminal. Percy, being a bit nosy, spotted some tablets which he assumed to be the slimming pills that kept people awake, especially Hamish, and made them talk nonsense.

Later that evening the hospital phoned to ask Percy to collect Hamish, who had woken up without being too much the worse for wear. Percy told Hamish very roundly he objected to being talked at by people under the influence of anything, and Hamish had better stop taking whatever it was. How well or how badly Hamish slept that night Percy had no idea, but thought rather fondly of Jet whose drunkenness and pretensions seemed more manageable. Hamish was tired and subdued the next morning. How he coped with his lessons Percy wasn't sure, but perhaps a less manic approach went down well. Hamish found some new digs where a large neutered tomcat would jump on his lap, but didn't scratch or bite. As for the Townsends, the whole incident was very much, "Mum's the word," and Mrs Townsend threw out all the medicaments she could find in the bathroom cabinet and pantry back shelf.

Chapter Seventeen

Arms and the Man

Although the translation of Metcalfe to a higher form and a corresponding relegation had not actually been announced in assembly, everybody seemed to know the full details of Mr Rowntree's promise of good behaviour, made to secure the dropping of the charge against him; but whatever sniggering went on behind his back, nobody showed him less than that accustomed terror which can never amount to genuine respect. It is perhaps one of life's great pities that teachers who deserve respect are sometimes treated with contempt or taken advantage of, whilst others, over-fearful of contempt or naturally dictatorial, may well keep order, but will never be liked. However, as was once said, "Let them hate me so long as they fear me." Mr Rowntree carried on intimidating his pupils without pointing rulers in their faces or setting unnecessary lines. But his victims had their consolation in his humiliation.

Mick Baxter had not had the misfortune to be taught Latin by Mr Rowntree in the junior school. He had not been kept on his feet, as the many and varied forms of Latin verbs and nouns were turned into instruments of torture. He had been taught by Mrs Thompson. That is not to say she was all sweetness and light. Her kindly nature and instinctive sense of humour were frequently masked by feigned or real savagery of the kind boys could cope with happily, reminding them as it did of their mothers. Old Ma Thompson was on the warpath again in the manner of the entire female sex. Mick had evolved from being cheeky and giggling all the time to having a level of interest in Latin that went beyond the hard graft of the language itself to those rarefied pastures where the gods of antiquity walked. It was a shame that, unlike his younger friend, Tim Russell, he had had to study physics and not Greek.

Mr Rowntree, detecting Mrs Thompson's fondness for Mick Baxter, had sought to undermine him in her eyes, criticising his walk, movement, facial expressions etc, and particularly his friendship with Tim Russell. In a strange mood of exasperation or protectiveness, poisoned perhaps by the toxic tobacco fumes of the staffroom, she had turned on Mick Baxter, as if telling him to be more self-aware, and not make silly faces. It was unfortunate this all came as rather an onslaught and naturally elicited the expression used to denote reeling under the slings and arrows. "There, you're doing it again," she said, storming off. She had included the remark, "we were talking about you," in her preamble, without making it clear she meant Mr Rowntree, and not her pipe-smoking, chess-playing colleagues. But Baxter had been spoiling for a fight with Smarticus, and had no doubt who she meant. Baxter had no intention of trying to look hard or walk with a swagger to prove anything to anybody.

Baxter's image of Jocelyn Alexis Rowntree, otherwise known as Smarticus, was of an uninspiring little tyrant who always wore the same houndstooth jacket; sported a large golden wedding ring attesting to his uxoriousness, which, being slightly too large, used to swivel round his finger, needing constant adjustment; unaccountably used a blue ball-point pen for marking, rather than red; and never lost his board duster. He may have acquired a military bearing somewhere along the line, but displayed no athleticism or muscularity, and instinctively sat at his desk, rather than delivering lessons from a standing position. He had a slight muscular weakness in his right eye, which would blink from time to time quite independently of his left eye. This was said to have been a lasting effect of an attack of Bell's palsy, purportedly sustained when one form had stuck pins in a voodoo likeness. Whatever the truth of the rumour, why this man should pontificate on carriage, deportment and facial expression was a mystery, as indeed was his National Service.

The upper sixth Latin class had almost completed their trek through Cicero's *Pro Milone*, without a word of explanation as to the subject matter, background or context, and hardly the need for any help in the translation, as the class members simply read him the turgid rendering of the crib they had concealed in the pages of the text. Mr Rowntree may have had some justification in that they were only required in the A-level examination to translate a piece into idiomatic, but accurate English, though he might have attempted to improve their literary style. But little or no comment or explanation was required on the content. Why should natural curiosity be allowed to waste the time available? The class had simply followed its leader without demur. However, when the final sentence had been construed, Baxter said rather sharply, "What was all that about, sir?"

"If you don't know, you've been wasting your time, and I will see to it that you stop your studies. He then picked up the first book of Virgil's *Aeneid* and read out the immortal lines, "Arma virumque cano."

He thought about concocting a story to the headmaster that Baxter should be forced to drop Latin, but didn't think the headmaster would oblige.

The classmates were divided in their opinion. Some had a sneaking admiration for Mr Rowntree's tyranny, others an admiration for Baxter for standing up to it. But Baxter wasn't entirely popular. He made his colleagues feel uncomfortable, as he challenged behavioural norms and attitudes, and wouldn't play the game.

Chapter Eighteen

The Second World War

Mr Townsend and Captain Turpin had jointly devised a discussion topic for the weekly sixth-form R.I. lessons, based on the Second World War. It was supposed to explore the issue of historical interpretation. Was there an official version of events which swept controversy under the carpet? Mr Townsend's view was that the discussion and research might be of use to the history students applying to Oxford or Cambridge, and at the same time would give him an opportunity to display his vast wealth of knowledge. The captain had been talked into it, and felt it was as good a subject as any for discussion. There were a core group of three or four who were the only ones ever to volunteer an opinion in his lessons, sometimes referred to as the "creeping death," and the captain was adept at shutting up anyone whose opinions disagreed with his own or ridiculing them. Meantime, he liked to broadcast his own at great length.

What spawned off from the lessons was a lunchtime debate, "This house believes that in the Second World War British governments recklessly sacrificed British lives." It promised to be good, and there was quite a high turn-out. Tim Russell was speaking for the proposition, and Percy attended with Mr Duvivier and Mr Sweet. Mr Townsend came in after them and sat at the back.

Tim pointed out that there were two wars, one in Europe, which included the Middle East, and one in the Far East. He was going to deal with the war in the Far East first, because it resulted entirely from the United Kingdom's acquisition of an overseas empire and its failure to relinquish it. Administration of the colonies was outdoor relief for the upper classes, its protection, a way of life for the officers. Against a determined foe such as the Japanese, who were surely as entitled as the British to have an empire, they could offer only token resistance. British lives were sacrificed on the battlefield and the work camps, constructing the bridge on the River Kwai and the Burma railroad. His mother's brother came home from the Japanese concentration camps a broken man. It was the Americans who defeated the Japanese in pursuit of their own imperial aims, and that only with the help of the bomb.

But turning to Europe, it was clearly apparent nothing could be done to stop the Germans marching into Austria, Czechoslovakia and Poland. To declare war on them for their invasion of Poland was an act of reckless folly. Why pick a fight you can't win? This was not to say that rearmament wasn't vital, but then was not the time for the war. Following the invasion of the Low Countries and France, possibly triggered by the declaration of war, Great Britain was lucky to recover most of its troops at Dunkirk. A subsequent option to sue for peace was not considered. Churchill sacrificed British lives on a deadly scale, recklessly seeking victories to console the British people for bombing, rationing and loss of life. There were the Arctic convoys, during which his father's brother went down aboard merchant ship SS *Scottish Trader*. There was horrendous loss of life in the North Africa campaigns, and operation Pedestal in 1942 to get petrol to Malta was, with the loss of life, only a token victory. His father nearly went down aboard H.M.S. *Lightning* in that operation, and was perhaps lucky to survive the war at all with damaged hearing from the guns and a permanent bad back from when the Lightning finally sank in March 1943 and time was spent in the cold sea. Admittedly, the Mediterranean isn't as cold as the North Sea or the Arctic Ocean. How much consolation this was when there wasn't enough room on the raft, and the better swimmers had to take their turn in the water, he didn't know. All this was said to be of the

117

greatest strategic importance, though one doubts it. We went to war for Poland, but as we know, an iron curtain descended across Europe, and we were in a cold war of indefinite duration.

The opposition took the view that Nazism was so totally repugnant, as evidenced by the concentration camps and destruction of European Jewry, that it had been a sacred duty to oppose it *ab initio*. Churchill had recognised the need for early re-armament and decisive firm action to deal with Hitler long before 1939. Churchill indeed recognised the moral imperative of continuing the struggle by whatever means possible. Churchill subsequently sought to go to active war with the Soviet Union for the liberation of Eastern Europe. We were reminded of the failure to do that with the invasion of Hungary and the building of the Berlin Wall.

The debate therefore raged from pure pragmatism to moral imperative. There were too many ifs and buts. The British people had accepted the sacrifices imposed on them, and if Hitler had not invaded Russia, nor Germany declared war on America, the Low Countries and France would be German controlled to this day, and the Mediterranean, an Italian lake. The motion was lost, and there was a round of applause for the late Winston Churchill, the greatest ever Englishman, the greatest ever Briton. Tim Russell's criticism of Churchill was regarded as little short of blasphemous.

Chapter Nineteen

Julius Caesar

Meanwhile Mr Tourtel was pressing on with his production of Julius Caesar. He was, as usual, unflappable. Respecting boys' needs to get home for their tea and to do their homework, he pared rehearsals to the bone. For lead parts he had an instinct for finding boys who could easily learn their lines. He was less concerned with their acting ability, and sometimes indifferent to the physical unsuitability of many a cast member. But most of all, he had the utmost faith in the costumes hired out by Nellie Smith's Nottingham Theatrical Supplies. Not everybody shared his views. The deputy head was scathing about that Nancy Price and her glad rags, as he used to remark in his more jocular moments, unwitnessed though they were by television cameras. He hadn't of course offered to help Mr McKenzie make them in his five-year spell at the school. Not that Mr McKenzie needed help from such a forlorn source after befriending the art master, and turning the art room into a workshop for costume manufacture.

Sidney Smith, the art master, was heavily set with hair growing on the top of his nose and a mouth of pock-marked teeth. He was prone to rant and rave about boys trampling in the bushes that bordered the crowded path running past the canteen, though it didn't seem to do the bushes any harm and speeded entry and exit. His foulest imprecations, however, were reserved for those boys who'd removed the rubber fittings from the chair legs that reduced the noise level emitted when they scraped across the floor. It was only one particular year that had been so diabolically motivated, but the missing rubbers had never been replaced. Whether the removed rubbers had been ceremonially displayed in trophy cabinets or thrown away was never discovered. In concert with the woodwork master, Wilf Bailey, he was engaged in a bitter war of attrition with the headmaster over the school's dismissive treatment of arts and crafts in the timetable. Only the lowest form was allowed to take them, in lieu of German or Latin, and to O-level only. Art was the most academic of subjects in Sidney's opinion, and he longed to teach it at A-level. However, neither of the two had ever gone so far as applying to teach at some other school where their talents might have been better appreciated, perhaps for fear they might not have had such an easy life.

Wilf Bailey, who had driven two motor cars into the same tree, at different times, in the course of learning to drive, had a vision of the bigger picture. The world would firstly be saved by contributions to the gift fund, however modest, and secondly by sixth form boys visiting old people deemed to be lonely by the local social services department. He committed himself to the organisation of such projects. This was different from the dispensation of universal salvation from the art room, by way of costumes glued with Copydex.

The important question was, when it came to the construction of sets, should the dramatic society seek first the assistance of the woodwork master or the art master? The dramatic society had over the years acquired a collection of tools, variously kept in a storeroom at the back of the stage and the art room. But set constructors eyed with envy the collection of tools in the woodwork room. There was no way the woodwork master would even lend them out under signature. Wilf's higher loyalties were to his tools, not the school play. Thus, he lost any control or involvement in set construction.

Mr McKenzie and Mr Smith were at variance from the rest of the staff in an important respect. They both lived in Central London and commuted the opposite direction to the suburban dwellers. They lived on the fringe of theatreland and liked to think they moved occasionally in theatrical circles. School plays, they thought, should jump through that magic hoop which turned them into great art. Others thought this was an unlikely result from or justification for all the work involved in making costumes, extra rehearsals and exotic lighting changes, requiring hours of practice. In the inordinate length of *Dr Faustus* Mr McKenzie had shot his bolt. Mr Tourtel now had a free hand, and relied little on the support of the art room.

But the art master was still free to comment from the side. Was Baxter a suitable Mark Antony? Was Tim Russell really right for Brutus? The set was unimaginative. Mrs Thompson and Mrs Tourtel did any necessary repairs to the hired costumes, and Mr Sweet, volunteering his services in applying make-up, lectured on Zen Buddhism as he slapped on Number 5 and Number 9. Percy entered the dressing room with Elizabeth shortly before the start of the Saturday evening performance. They were honoured by the guest appearance of Captain Turpin, who appeared to have been drinking spirits all afternoon. He was in a high good humour, and wearing a fine buff and brown sports jacket. He was anxious to wish everybody good luck, and tell a few privileged ears about the time he'd played Mark Antony. Baxter somehow pre-empted the headmaster with an adroit manoeuvre. "What a super sports jacket, sir. Can I touch it for luck?"

The captain was genuinely chuffed, but said he doubted he had the royal touch. Fortunately, there wasn't so much scrofula about these days. He then quite forgot his intended reminiscences and pointers as to delivery of the lines. As he lurched off, Mr Tourtel muttered under his breath, "Break a leg." No doubt he wasn't the only one who wished the captain would.

Percy and Elizabeth greatly enjoyed the play. During the interval they spoke to Mr Sweet, who claimed to have been raised on the play by his grandmother, and Mr Barker, a French teacher, who was lamenting he'd been talked into going on the school's Easter trip to Paris. Mr Montgomery, the French head, who organised the trip every year, expected him to attend meetings each lunch time, when every last second of the trip was allocated with the utmost precision to an exhausting series of outings. "I've had enough of the trip even before it's started. What a conceited nitwit that man is."

Percy thought it a neat description of most members of the staff.

Chapter Twenty

The Evans Family

It was often said of Elizabeth's father, Richard Evans, he was a most intelligent man, an expression usually denoting the man in question was at best laconic, at worst, singularly dull company. In relation to Richard, however, it was apologetic for his being sharp-tongued, prejudiced and anti-social. Whether the anti-social side of his character came from deep-seated shyness or fear of ridicule was uncertain. He sometimes came over as slightly effeminate in his mannerisms or tones, though there was no evidence he was in the least bit homosexual. Queers, however, were high on his list of bêtes noires, along with all of a darker hue, Gypsies, Jews, the Irish and women drivers. He could be quite charming and witty, though devastatingly rude about colleagues, relations, neighbours and in-laws, behind their backs. His long attempts to control and isolate his wife had been doomed to failure, due to the amount of money she made.

He had a naval background, and a flare for ship design was soon demonstrated at nautical training school. When he met her, his future wife, Lily Blake, was a seamstress, daughter of a master-tailor. She put his potential career in the Royal Corps of Naval Constructors above his possessiveness, and allowed him to wean her off the local tennis club she had struggled so long to join. They married shortly before the outbreak of the Second World-War. Their oldest son, Alex, was born in 1940, Brian, in 1941, and Elizabeth, in 1943.

With the evacuation to Bath of the Director of Naval Construction, they settled in that area. Lily had always had a talent for telling stories, and soon took advantage of finding domestic help to spend a few hours a day scribbling. Richard might well have thought his wife should have been slaving over a hot stove, but his colleagues' wives all had home help, sat on committees and socialised. Slaving over a typewriter at least kept her indoors. Besides, she was soon earning money. She didn't perhaps have a great deal to say. She soon ran out of children's stories based on her own childhood and that of her own children, but then turned to Mills and Boon type fiction. Her love stories might not have been as good as her children's stories, but she could churn them out, and they sold.

They were earning a lot of money between them, and it seemed sensible to purchase the final seven years of a lease on a flat in Bayswater. They could stay in town, when she travelled up to meet her publishers, and could drag Richard along to the theatre, where they might pass off as cosmopolitans, intellectuals and patrons of the arts. It would give him something to tell his despised colleagues, and of course, the children might need a place in town.

The boys were as different as chalk and cheese. Alex was naturally scruffy and in a perpetual dream. He walked with one foot on the pavement and one in the gutter, scuffing his shoes. He hardly knew what a comb was for. Brian was instinctively smart, a natural swank, methodical, tidy and organised. Both, however, were braggarts. For all that Brian applied himself much better to school work, Alex had more basic intelligence, but chose to waste it.

A service tradition running in the family, Richard thought it was the Merchant Navy for Alex and the Royal Air Force for Brian. It wasn't clear what Lily thought or whether she even cared. She was used to fighting her corner with her husband, wanting to get on with her writing and attend the odd literary lunch or radio interview; but really, it wasn't such a bad idea to get the boys out of the house. They were only in the way, after all. She hadn't quite sacrificed them. Had they come to her saying they wanted to go on the stage, she might have backed them. She didn't see either of them as solicitors, bank managers or estate agents, and provided they weren't having to swing a pick-axe, wasn't much concerned. Elizabeth was the clever one, and she could be the one to study. She even played the piano.

Brian prospered in the RAF, but was inclined to run up mess bills, which his father sorted out, as he could well afford to. Alex spent rather less. The booze on board ship was all duty-free, and there was an endless supply of slimming tablets to keep the toper awake, and ensure a semblance of normality the following day. He was soon habituated to pills, and found plentiful supplies in the pubs and drinking clubs of Bath, where there was always someone he had to see. He would come home, and try to interest his father in strange investments, such as snail farming. He always knew people with unlikely businesses for sale or requiring capital. He was a great hit with the ladies, and soon had one in the family way. The flat in London was just the place for an early forced marriage. His wife, Judy, wanted him out of the Merchant Navy, resenting being left on her own with her son, Jimmy, when he was on a booze cruise. He found jobs as sales representatives. He could take pills, shout his mouth off, and clinch a few deals. In his eyes he was a successful business man. Not so in Judy's eyes. He could never make enough to suit her. A second child was born, a daughter Alice, but the marriage was unravelling fast, with his drunken behaviour and her constant nagging. Alex was negotiating a loan to purchase a new lease on the flat, but even as he did, she had planned her escape. Was her new partner the real father of Alice? Alex had by now lost his job and was attempting to make a living as a drug dealer. There followed a drug raid, a term of imprisonment and action to repossess the flat. The money

125

borrowed at a high rate to purchase the lease had been the working capital of his business, and there wasn't much left.

It all proved a gift to his mother, however. There were several novels there, and it sparked off her desire to move to Central London. She had never really liked the countryside, and the delights of Bath had long worn off. With nothing to do in the Royal Corps of Naval Constructors, the government obstinately refusing to order ships in peacetime, her husband was talked into the idea of early retirement, moving to London and being able to house Alex in the basement or garden shed, until he was back on his feet.

Percy was invited to stay in Bath for the Easter holidays, but subject to helping with some of the clearance for the move to London. Also, they were to visit Aunty Wynnie, to do whatever they could to help her. Brian might well appear who was stationed at Brize Norton.

Percy didn't want the Townsends to know he was travelling to Bath with Elizabeth, and drove off on Sunday 3rd April as if heading in the direction of Truro, but instead turned off to pick up Elizabeth. They then found the way round the South Circular to the Chiswick flyover and M4. They were soon chugging along in the slow lane, not daring to go too fast for fear of the noise levels, overheating or that the car might simply drop to bits. A Morris Minor had its limits after all. It was a relief to re-join the A4 after bypassing Maidenhead.

Bathnorton was an attractive village, with a wonderful olde worlde pub. The Evanses' two-storey house was large, comfortable and modern. What it lacked in charm, despite some expensive oak panelling in the hall, it made up for in practicality. The downstairs facility was no mere W.C. It was a cloakroom to die for. Pride of place in the front sitting room was Richard's antique writing desk. At the rear were separate doors to the imposing dining-room and the well-appointed kitchen, but the two rooms adjoined, and both opened into a fine conservatory. The dining room was big enough for both dining-room and lounge suites. Upstairs were four bedrooms, one of which had been taken over as Lily's study, the star attraction of which was the latest electric typewriter, which she addressed as either Algy or Bertie, out of a fondness for the Biggles stories of W. E. Johns. The Evanses determinedly slept in the same bed; so when Elizabeth was staying, there was still a spare bedroom, occupied the previous Christmas by Aunty Wynnie. Lily didn't approve of anyone sleeping on settees, and was relieved neither of the boys had shown up.

There was an exquisite rose bed round a modest lawn, and each summer Mr Evans grew raspberries and runner beans, and in a tiny greenhouse nurtured his tomatoes. You might have been forgiven for thinking, as Percy did, that this was the nearest you could get to earthly paradise, and why on earth did the Evanses wish to move to London; but they professed themselves Londoners at heart. Lily was set on a Georgian house in a grand street, somewhere really central, such as Islington. Even Greenwich would be the sticks. Percy could only think of his favourite character from fiction, Mr Pooter, whose *Diary of a Nobody* was set in nearby Holloway, his house, The Laurels. Percy wasn't much impressed.

They were plied with large glasses of dry sherry before dinner. It was an expensive sherry, but not to Percy's taste. Elizabeth sipped but slowly. Firstly, she didn't want a drink anyway, but secondly resented the fact that her father begrudged giving her a drink. In his eyes drinking was for the chaps, and administering alcohol to ladies was always with an ulterior motive. In the normal course of events he poured an abstemious glass for his wife, Lily, purely because he didn't want to be a solitary drinker; but kept topping his own up when he thought she wasn't looking.

Richard soon moved on to his job in the constructors' corps. There was no war on and no demand for ships. That was the pity of it all. He was profoundly disappointed in his career, and sometimes felt utterly worthless. He didn't say that he was, nevertheless, exceedingly well-paid for doing nothing, and how good it was there was no war going on. He had a keen interest in naval history, and had always kept a diary, like Samuel Pepys, his hero. When they moved to London he was going to write. He had plans.

Mrs Evans was interesting. She was extremely shrewd and highly intelligent, but had lacked anything beyond elementary education: no algebra, no French, little English literature. She had left school at fourteen, worked in the rag trade, learnt to sew after a fashion, sold hats, and looked for a husband she felt was going places. Her publishers sent her copies of what was selling elsewhere, anything they thought might give her ideas, and out of it all she spun her own material. It might be thought that invention was the essential pre-requisite for a fiction writer, but Elizabeth had hinted that her mother believed her own lies. This was perhaps apparent as she got on to the subject of her sons: how Brian was doing so well in the RAF, what a brilliant career was opening up, what a success he was with the ladies, the hearts he had broken; of Alex, how unlucky he had been with his diabolically scheming wife who had bled him dry and encouraged him to seek easy ways of making money. First, she ruined him, now she restricted his access to the children. Lily was thus deprived of her rights and would never see her grandchildren.

It was perhaps apparent that Elizabeth had heard all this so often, she would seek any excuse to get away. She suggested Percy might like to go to The Swan, and he nodded, thinking it could hardly be any less smoky. If the Evanses had a religion, it was Embassy tipped.

They sat quietly holding hands in the pub. It would be nice to be married and have their own home. "I don't know if mother is hinting that, when they've moved to Islington, or wherever, I could live with them. I don't think I could bear it."

It was apparent to Percy that Elizabeth wasn't quite as fond of her parents as dutiful adult children should be. By the time they got back from the pub the Evanses were both in bed.

Chapter Twenty-One

A trip to Weston-super-Mare

Mr Evans was an early riser. He usually nodded off of an evening, downing a few gins on his favourite sofa, then woke up and smoked a pipe of tobacco, pontificating meanwhile on his favourite subjects, such as the demerits of the working-class, trade unionists, coloured immigrants, white immigrants etc. Mrs Evans, who sipped her gins at a much slower rate, was always preoccupied with the plot of her next pot-boiler, but gave the impression she was not only listening, she was hanging on every word. She couldn't actually stand his views at all, but was grateful to him for having rescued her from a life of real or imaginary poverty, and having given her the chance to write.

After his pipe of tobacco, he would sip a glass of brandy, and nod off again. Mrs Evans would then go to bed. Waking up with a start, he would observe the empty space where his wife had been sitting, deduce she had gone on ahead of him, and follow her up. As soon as his head touched the pillow, he would fall asleep, even though his wife was reading a book and shamelessly smoking in bed. He would then wake up before six and take an extended bath, waiting for his wife to make tea and toast. If the tea and toast weren't ready precisely when he emerged from his ablutions in yellow terry-towelling bath-robe, he would dress in one of his many heavy woollen suits, before heading for the breakfast table. When he was in luck, the newsagent's boy would have delivered a copy of the *Telegraph*, whose politics he agreed with, whilst knowing full well there was a copy of *The Times* in the office for a less biased view of the world.

Elizabeth maintained her father was not to be disturbed at such time and they should time their appearance till they heard him shut the front door rather loudly and start up his 3.5 litre Rover. So they did that the first morning, but Percy realised Elizabeth was spoiling for a fight with her mother on any subject whatsoever, and he should keep his silence. "I'll go and check the levels in the car," he said. When he got back, the plan was they should phone Aunty Wynnie's neighbour to inform her of the visit and stop her from going off to the old people's day centre, where she wasn't always the most welcome visitor.

Percy was glad to be on the road to the recalcitrant aunt, but shocked by the neglect, filth and rampant hoarding that awaited him when he got there. On the positive side, she was in good health, and had definitely recovered from what was only a very slight apoplectic fit rather than a major cerebrovascular accident She was very pleased to see her niece with such a nice young man, though a bit apprehensive they were going to start tidying up. Percy suggested to Elizabeth that they took her out for the day. "How about fish and chips in Minehead?" he suggested. The proposition was put to Wynnie who thought it a wonderful idea, and put on her oldest raincoat, as it looked a touch inclement. The look of the raincoat did not deter her. Elizabeth smiled. Her mother would have been appalled; her father, merely dismissive. She was his aunt, after all.

The distance from Weston-super-Mare to Minehead is about forty-five miles. Elizabeth was rather good at navigating, and suggested they took the coast road to Burnham-on-Sea, joined the main road to Bridgwater and then took the A39. She would navigate from the back seat, so Wynnie could sit in pride of place at the front of the car eagerly taking in the view. In point of fact, however, Wynnie did not just nod off discreetly, she snored loudly in complete oblivion. Margaret did her best to wake her up when she thought the scenery particularly interesting, but neither the Quantock nor Brendon Hills excited her imagination sufficiently to raise an eyebrow.

On arrival they parked near the sea front, explored the Blenheim Gardens, and looked round St Michael's Church and the old railway terminus, before heading to a fish-and-chips restaurant.

Aunty insisted on paying for the meal, loudly extolling the virtues of the place, the food, her niece and intended. Her rather shabby handbag, which matched her rather shabby raincoat, seemed to contain a large percentage of her life savings, tucked away in its many pockets. Margaret and Percy pretended not to notice. Afterwards, they strolled a short distance towards the south-west, lamenting that it was too far to walk all the way to Porlock, before returning to the car. Aunty was strong in her protestations that it had been a wonderful outing, but she didn't mind sitting in the back, where she fell asleep instantly.

Waking up on return to Weston she insisted they drove to see her parish church of St Paul's Kewstoke. This entailed essaying Monks Hill with its one-in-four gradient. She walked the journey every Sunday, via the Monks Steps, which were cut into the side of the hill long before the road was constructed. Changing into first gear required the hill-start, an accomplishment still achieved by the locals in pre-war Austin 7s. Percy wasn't terribly amused.

Returning to her bungalow, she suggested they all called on the next-door neighbours for a cup of tea. The neighbours obliged with a wry grin, and seemed to be fond of her eccentric ways.

Travelling back in the car, they expressed regret they hadn't actually done anything to help clear the mess or assist Wynnie's living

132

arrangements; but on the other hand, they'd probably made the best compromise. Everyone likes an outing, after all, especially with fish and chips. Lily and Richard were intrigued by the account of the day. The evening meal of dressed crab was not very substantial. It was therefore fortunate that Percy and Elizabeth had dined well midday. Afterwards, they sat having intellectual conversation over large gin and tonics, whilst Mr and Mrs Evans manically smoked Embassy Tipped. Percy couldn't help noticing the gift coupon catalogue on the coffee table, wondering how many you needed for an iron lung.

The following day they dutifully kept out of the way until Mr Evans had driven off to work. Percy then suggested he went out to buy a paper, in order to give Elizabeth a chance to quarrel with her mother, but at that moment the *Telegraph* was delivered late.

The daily woman, Mrs Giddings, normally called about 9.45. Lily usually liked to have washed up the breakfast dishes to ease the load on poor Mrs Giddings who was expected to cook a main meal for 1.15 pm when Richard came home for lunch, as well as follow her cleaning routines. She was expected to wash up after lunch, and usually attempted to do the ironing while her lord and lady dined, or finished off the dusting.

The evening meal prepared by Lily about six p.m. was less formal, less substantial, and described as high tea. Elizabeth offered to get it ready that afternoon, being told it should be a salad with tinned salmon. Although there was a weekly delivery of groceries, there was, nevertheless, a lengthy shopping list pinned up on a notice board in the kitchen. This was handed to Elizabeth who was informed they should be back for lunch, Mrs Giddings having been told to cook for four. With the shopping they wouldn't have time to look round Bath, but could go back out after lunch, provided they returned in time to prepare tea. Elizabeth and Lily then proceeded to row about the proposed move to London, but Lily got very short with her daughter. "My girl, when I want your advice, I'll ask for it." When they were in the car, Lily exploded. "They're both short of breath from all that smoking. What do they want to move to a five-storey house for? Here they have nice-sized rooms. In the new house cramped rooms will be separated by endless stairs and hallways. They will have a kitchen diner in the back basement room, too small for their suite. The front basement utility/storeroom will contain a single bed for Alex. 'How good I am towards him,' she will say. 'Let down and abandoned by wife and friends, I alone have a room for him.' Of course, there won't be any room for his possessions and he'll be debarred from the rest of the house. Whether she'll pretend not to notice what he smokes, or indeed won't notice, is not clear. What will father do all day? He can get a typist to type up his diaries and give them to the Imperial War Museum. I can't see him writing a book. He'll be doing crosswords and listening to The Navy Lark."

The withering contempt rather amused Percy. They found somewhere to park at vast expense and went for a stroll; but the requirement to do the shopping and return hung over them like a heavy sentence, precluding the delights of coffee and a cake. Mr Evans had beaten them back, and the meal was about to be served. It was roast lamb with frozen peas and instant mashed potato, followed by a home-made apple pie and ice cream. Percy couldn't help noticing Richard kept getting up and denouncing iniquity, whilst re-filling his glass from the sherry decanter. He didn't seem in much hurry to return to the office, he strongly recommended the assembly rooms and the waters, and talked vaguely about going to the theatre, if anything was on, which they could find out. They waited for Mr Evans to go, and were then told Mrs Giddings had gone, and they were to do the washing up.

They just about managed to see the designated tourist sites before coming back to prepare the meal. Elizabeth apologised for the regimentation. Richard was already home solving the crossword puzzle with the help of a glass of sherry and cigarette. They had forgotten about the theatre programme, as indeed had Richard. That evening they suggested they all went to The Swan, but fortunately Richard and Lily declined. With a sense of relief Percy and Elizabeth left one smoky venue for another, where Liz encountered an old school friend with her newly married husband. They chatted mainly about house prices and mortgages.

On Wednesday, Lily was distinctly frosty, as if Percy had already outstayed his welcome; but in truth she had heard the previous evening that Flight Officer Brian Evans was likely to be honouring his parents with a visit. He took preference over a mere future son-in-law, and for once wasn't bringing one of his many attractive, but fleeting, girl-friends. Plans were revised. Percy would drive on Maundy Thursday to Truro, taking Elizabeth to meet his parents. She would return to Bath by train on Saturday. Percy would travel back to Bath on Easter Monday and drive Elizabeth to Kent with all her remaining possessions from the parental home. She would thus be obliged to throw substantial amounts out, Lily being adamant that none of Elizabeth's worldly goods (Mrs Evans couldn't quite bring herself to say "stuff") were to go in the furniture van to Islington, when the contentious move took place. Sorting it out would give Elizabeth something to do on Easter Sunday, and stop her doing anything silly like going to church, even if only for the music.

Percy had the great privilege of shaking hands with the flying officer before commencing the drive to Truro. Percy's parents were much taken with Elizabeth, and more accommodating over the sleeping arrangements than hers were. There weren't clouds of smoke everywhere, nor were they tyrannised by the meal arrangements. It wasn't perhaps apparent to Elizabeth that Mrs Spenser was on her best behaviour, or rather less neurotic than usual; but Mrs Spenser was both charmed and calmed by Elizabeth, though only up to a point. She was prone to blow hot and cold about people, usually in the same sentence.

Chapter Twenty-Two

Strong Cocktails

Percy awoke early that Good Friday in a foul humour. He donned all his previous day's clothes, crept out of the house, and headed off for a walk in the woods, despite it being barely light, and not having a dog to exercise. Somehow, he was seething. He had had enough of his girl-friend, her parents, his parents, the Morris Minor, digs at the Townsends, Bury's Ancient History, Alexis Rowntree and so on. In his mind he had contemplated the two-mile hike to Idless Woods where he planned to wander all day; but in fact only got as far as the Victoria Gardens, before running out of steam, only to discover they were closed. The woods on the other side of the road beckoned, but more so when he thought he espied a familiar figure walking a poodle. "Could it be Felicity Sheridan?" he thought with some excitement. His heart beat a little faster. All his observations from the Christmas party came back to him. Her teeth were goofy, but surely that was attractive. She was earnest, shrill and feisty, all characteristics making her unsuitable for a long-term relationship; there were her sudden inexplicable outbursts, as she changed her mind about something entirely unknown to all around her; his father had told him to get stuck in, because she would be a bit of a goer. He remembered the excitement of kissing her, before his mother had spoiled everything by falling in the pond. It didn't take long to catch up with her. Her red duffle coat was unfastened, her breasts prominent under her white roll-neck jumper in chunky knit. Without compunction, they started snogging. The dog, which belonged to a neighbour who'd gone skiing, didn't seem to mind.

"Have you missed me?" she said provocatively.

"I've thought of you every day," he replied, lying through his teeth.

"I don't believe a word."

137

"Then why did you ask?"

"Just teasing. What are your plans?"

They sat on a fallen tree trunk, arranging the date to take place when Elizabeth returned to her parents. The Sheridans would be most obliging in such matters. It didn't actually seem respectable. Percy knew, whatever the outcome of the dalliance with Felicity, he had to break off his relationship with Elizabeth. He couldn't even say engagement, though they were engaged in all but name. He felt defeated, as if all passion had been drained out by the complications of being alone together. He understood you had to work at marriage, but having to work so hard at an unofficial engagement seemed most unfair, as well as exhausting. The dog grew restless, and they both needed to be home for breakfast; but the assignation had been organised. The difficult bit now lay ahead.

When he had returned to the house, his parents were both up, but not Elizabeth. He crept upstairs and entered the bedroom.

"Where have you been?" Elizabeth asked. Her tone was entirely neutral.

"I don't need your permission to go out for a walk."

"You might have asked me."

"But you were asleep."

"I'm only doing this for you."

"Doing what?"

"Visiting your parents."

"They're a great deal more obliging than yours."

"What do you mean by obliging?"

"Well, it isn't all Embassy tipped and single beds."

"I don't know what you mean."

"I don't know what's the matter with you."

"Your hearts not in this unofficial engagement and future marriage. Pretend all you like about a semi-detached and the choir we'll join."

138

"There'll be the amateur dramatics as well, *Hamlet*, *Hippolytus*, Hermia and Helena." Percy thought of Lysander (or was it Demetrius?) in *A Midsummer Night's Dream*, saying "Not Hermia, but Helena I love." Did he regret the tedious hours he had spent with Elizabeth?

"Don't be facetious," Elizabeth cut in.

Who was the last person to call him facetious? Percy thought it time for a direct approach. He grabbed Elizabeth by the arms, as if determined to have his wicked way with her; but she shook him off, and said rather dramatically, "You can only think of one thing."

Percy took this as a moot point. "I've only been able to think of one thing for at least the last ten years, though somehow managed O-levels, A-levels and a double first."

"You're so modest with it."

"Well, it's better than being tight-lipped."

"I'm going to have my bath."

"Take a shower. It uses less hot water." At that he walked off in search of a cup of coffee, if not a full English breakfast.

His mother was setting out the breakfast table in the dining room. She bitterly resented the idea of frying breakfasts to individual requirements, but equally objected to the requirement to wash heated serving dishes. In any event, the sideboard was decorated with ornaments and photographs, so there would have been nowhere to put them.

"Where's Elizabeth?" she said.

"Having a bath."

"Well, she should have come to breakfast in her dressing gown, and you need a shave. She's a nice girl, but there's no spunk in her."

"You've hardly met her."

"Don't argue."

139

As Percy's father had often said to him, "The trouble with women is you're always in the wrong." His mother's mood was the least of his worries. She would be charm itself before long. "Where's father?" "In the potting shed, doubtless having a secret snifter." "Well, I'll find out."

His father was in fact digging compost out of the bin and transferring it to a wheelbarrow. "She's a nice girl," he said. "Too nice for you. You both need nagging, and you're both too polite. I preferred that Sheridan girl." Percy was tempted to say you might well be right, but kept quiet. "Reckon it'll be another freezing cold Easter. They usually are. Did you know William's coming today? I think he's split up with his young lady. You'll have to keep Elizabeth out of his clutches, don't you know."

Percy didn't know what he either knew or didn't. The distinct possibility opened up that Elizabeth would be whisked out of his life painlessly. He might even claim to be the deeply wounded party, whilst shamelessly advancing his cause with Felicity. Percy lacked the necessary ruthlessness the earnest lover requires. The day's programme remained unsorted. Elizabeth had expressed an interest in church, but only if the music or singing were any good. This was a good excuse not to go. Margaret would naturally moan about the cooking, without a serious attempt at delegation. She was clearly going to do breakfast, but not lunch, and would do dinner, but not afternoon tea or supper. Albert's best suggestion was that Percy took Elizabeth for a long walk and then to the pub, which he reckoned would be open from 12.00 to 2.00. They should then come back, have a cheese sandwich and go to bed. Whether this was compatible with finishing with Elizabeth and starting with Felicity wasn't clear, but Albert wasn't party to his son's deliberations.

They went in to the house to survey the breakfast front, and sat down as Margaret waited on everyone, especially Elizabeth, who had come in refreshed from her bath, wearing a rather revealing dressing gown. Albert assumed a look of professional indifference. Margaret was excited by the prospect of William's arrival. Percy was in turmoil. They all ate hearty breakfasts, and Percy volunteered to do the washing up. There was no offer of assistance from Elizabeth, but rather she wanted to discuss her parents' medical problems with Albert. He listened with interest. They were beginning, she thought, to suffer from emphysema. As she put it, they were running out of puff, but didn't have smokers' coughs. Albert confirmed it was possible, and all the more insidious. Lungs could be damaged without the chronic bronchitis that would alert the dangers. But if they really wanted to move to a five-storey house, let them. No doubt they would be able sell at a substantial profit by the time they came to their senses; but meanwhile they would avoid suffering from bungalow legs, a condition characterised by complete atrophy of the leg muscles in consequence of having no stairs to climb up or down at all. Albert certainly couldn't see the point of moving to London if you weren't in the first flush of youth. There was traffic noise and air pollution, and how many street-markets, museums and theatres did anyone want to go to? Elizabeth was in agreement. She got on with Albert, and suddenly started opening up about her family and all its complications, even mentioning her brothers. Albert was fascinated. He really liked her, and felt happy to talk until they both ran out of steam. He hardly spoke to his wife, and not a lot to his sons. He had his old codgers in the pub, but pub conversation was entirely superficial, however animated.

Percy meanwhile had finished the washing up and felt he really didn't want to go for a long walk with Elizabeth. Her company was starting to grate and she no longer aroused him. Circumstances had conspired against them. One half of him felt very sorry for her and the act of betrayal he was contemplating, while the other half said, "All's fair in love and war." He couldn't really discuss it with his mother, since her opinions and moods swung so wildly. Like many a young man, he had no confidant and had drifted on a path allotted by fate. Certainly at Oxford he had got in with all the wrong people. He went into the garden and started digging out compost morosely in a mood of self-punishment and self-pity. He then glanced up to see a red MG Midget sports car screeching up the drive. It was William, and the accustomed mixture of conflicting resentment and affection surged through him. They had barely time to exchange pleasantries before Margaret came running out. William was the true love of her life, perhaps because he had so little time for her. But how come he was so early? He explained he'd been to a friend's place in Exeter, well on business really, and had left at the crack of dawn. His friend was trying to sell him the MG, and had suggested he tried it out. Percy wondered whether the friend would see either the car again or the money. He was rather envious of William for driving something more exciting than the Morris Minor, even if it were distinctly less practical. They all headed to the sitting room, joining Albert and Elizabeth. Percy offered to make everyone coffee.

One of his mother's prize possessions was a gold-coloured tea trolley. It was extremely useful for serving tea or coffee in the sitting room, though it was just the kind of item one's best friends would ridicule as being naff or petit bourgeois. Percy was curiously sensitive to criticism in matters of style. He wheeled the trolley in, noting that William was holding court and Elizabeth was hanging on every word. Percy served up coffee, but was hardly noticed. He went off for a quick shave and perfunctory wash, returned, and sat there uncomfortably, hoping for an entry into the conversation, but found none. He thought longingly of Felicity and his date the following evening, after Elizabeth had gone in the morning. But he still had to take Elizabeth and her "stuff" back to Kent. Could he get out of that? He didn't believe she had anything very much that her parents couldn't take to their new London home. He sat there in a kind of daze, disgusted by his own fickleness and dishonesty. He was then surprised to hear William offering to drive her to Bath. There was a friend in Bath he wanted to see. Percy couldn't help butting in with the comment that he surely had to go back to Exeter to pay for the car or return it.

"You can be so boring, Percy," William replied. Percy took the opportunity to walk out, leaving the tea trolley behind. He went into the garden to look for something to do. The flower beds were full of bulbs. Random digging and turning of the soil were thus contra-indicated. The lawn, however, looked just dry enough to cut with the old hand mower. Percy had never got on with its petrol replacement. Brute force and ignorance were his instinctive tools for lawn-mowing. To his surprise, the old mower's blades had been reground and the mechanism oiled. It cut like a dream. Nobody had mentioned the overhaul, but it seemed more likely his mother had found someone to do it, despairing of the petrol mower she so disliked, which Dr Spenser would neither fix himself nor get serviced; but then he always left everything for her to do anyway.

The exercise did Percy good. Briefly, he forgot all his cares and woes, as he almost got stripes in the lawn. But then he looked up from his not quite hard labour to espy Elizabeth and William, the latter of whom assured Percy he was doing a grand job.

"I'm glad you think so," said Percy in a rather neutral guarded fashion. "It's all down to this new lawn-mower, or rather mower from the ark." There was a limit to how long lawn-mowers could sustain the conversation.

"However Elizabeth is getting to Bath tomorrow, how shall we best entertain her today?"

"Tennis," Willian said decisively. "The club's probably open, and there's the public court."

"Have we got any kit, and don't we need a fourth?"

"What about the Sheridan girl?"

"I don't know."

"Well, I'm going to ring her up," William stated defiantly, and marched off, leaving Percy embarrassed. The tips of his ears turned red.

"Oh, who's the Sheridan girl?" Elizabeth inquired.

Percy was baffled by his brother's knowledge of Felicity and not above the occasional half-truth.

"The Sheridans are nouveau rich arrivistes, patients of my father, but not private patients. They have a daughter at Sussex University, who William fancies. But then he fancies every girl, chats them up shamelessly and abandons them. Like Theseus and Ariadne." (Percy always thought classical allusions were a great help in conversation.)

"Have you got anything you could play in?"

"You'd be surprised!"

Percy thought perhaps he was rediscovering desire for Elizabeth, as they skated on such thin ice.

"A skimpy skirt."

"To match your short tight shorts."

At that moment William reappeared.

"You're a dark horse, Percy. You must have known the Sheridans have a tennis court in their garden. After all, you went to their Christmas party, didn't you?"

"What time are we playing?" Percy asked firmly, attempting command of the situation.

"Half-past two," William said. "I'm sure you can amuse yourselves till then. I'm having a lie down. Felicity reckons she's got some kit."

"Let's go for a walk," Percy suggested to Elizabeth, without much conviction. "We could go to church," Elizabeth replied enigmatically, "Or rather the cathedral."

"Most certainly." Percy was inclined to forget the existence of the magnificent work of Victorian architecture located in what the guidebooks described as a thriving Cornish city. It was agreed. They went, looked round, listened to part of a service, and returned to cheese sandwiches in the kitchen. William appeared shortly before their due time to depart in a stylish track suit. Percy felt somehow inferior to his brother for never having owned a tracksuit. Elizabeth seemed hardly aware. Her mind was definitely elsewhere. She could be so difficult, Percy reflected; and advanced it as a reason for replacing her with Felicity, if that was what he really wanted, having the feeling it wasn't. William exuded confidence as to rackets, tennis balls and anything you might play in, though the weather was getting colder. Percy drove them round to the Sheridans. Felicity answered the door seeming both bubbly and silly. Was she really up for tennis?

"I've had a look at the court," she said, "it's like hopeless, not in any fit state, don't you need nets, and it's not cool, baby. Well, yeah, one of you's Percy and one isn't. I can't tell, but you, you're Elizabeth. Hi." With that she kissed Elizabeth, who kissed her, and said, "Well are we coming in or not?"

"Follow me," she said, grabbing Elizabeth's hand and leading the way into the front reception room. She sat Elizabeth next to her on the settee and waved to the twins to sit where they liked.

"Sorry about the tennis, but it's too cold, and I'm no good anyway. The folks are up at the golf club with the silly dog. Drink anyone? I fancy mixing cocktails."

Nobody had been planning on an afternoon session, but it seemed a good idea. Felicity found a tea towel which gave the recipe for a number of deadly drinks. She sat with Elizabeth, engrossed in details of the Manhattan, Martini, Bloody Mary, the Mai Tai and the Whisky sour.

"Let's invent our own," suggested Elizabeth surprisingly. Felicity giggled. They got up, and rather ignoring the twins, examined the contents of the cocktail cabinet.

"Rum, lime juice and orange curaçao with almond syrup, or vodka and tomato juice with pepper and Worcester sauce," Felicity stated, eventually. "Come along boys, what's it to be?"

It reminded Percy somewhat of days at Oxford with Jet and dubious mixtures. He had a premonition that nothing would be quite the same again. In vino, veritas.

"I'll have the lot," said William.

"Are you sure that's wise?" Percy asked apprehensively.

"That's a good idea," said Felicity. "The ultimate gargle blaster. Are you game, Elizabeth?"

"Call me Liz, and yes I am."

The astonishing cocktails were then handed round, which promised to blow your head off. Only the most hardened alcoholic could swig such potent drinks without almost instant inebriation, but all the tomato juice, lemon juice, lime juice, orange curaçao and Worcester sauce somehow disguised the strength, luring the toper into rapid loss of inhibition and total collapse. It was perhaps fortunate they weren't in the garden by the pond.

"Here's to us," Percy ventured timidly.

"Oh, fuck us," said Elizabeth, "here's to Middle Earth!"

"Here's to Bilbo Baggins!" Fiona interjected.

"Hobbits are all wankers," said William.

"They're imaginary creatures," said Percy, about to summarise the works of Tolkien, but unable to remember a word. "Golly, gosh," he continued, "don't they eat two breakfasts and smoke St Bruno?"

"He's too smart for that," opined William.

146

"Who is?" said Elizabeth.

"St Bruno," William replied

"A pipe does something for a man," said Felicity.

"St Bruno does something more," said Elizabeth.

"What?" asked Percy.

"Gives him manly allure," Elizabeth replied. "But Percy, I wouldn't bother to start smoking it. What's nice about you is you don't have manly allure."

"You're dead right about that," said William, going for the jugular. "He's my fairy brother."

"But not only are you fairy similar. You're fairy identical." Having slurred these words, Felicity commenced hiccupping. "I'm going to be sick." She rose with a stagger and lurched off to the downstairs bathroom with Elizabeth in tow.

"Women are all lesbians," William said, as dogmatically as you possibly could when so drunkenly slurring your words. "At least, they are a bit. They become very girly, have anti-men phases, and cuddle up to each other, especially when drunk. Either you want to give them a good shagging, or you don't. You can't have honourable intentions. You've been kidding yourself, experimenting with a view to conformity and a bourgeois life style. Give it up. They're not for you."

Percy was a bit aghast to have the truth spoken so graphically, a truth he had tried to suppress for so long, a truth revealed to him by the one person who might know him the best. At the same time, he was so awfully drunk he felt he was floating on a cloud above it all and need never come down to earth to confront anything or anybody. But slowly the realisation trickled down to him that Elizabeth had guessed all along, and maybe she was experimenting too. He'd had doubts as to her sincerity, and been deterred by her lukewarm interest and apparent

147

absence of commitment. There would be no suburban semi-detached, no church choir, no children growing up and calling him "Daddy." But there'd be all those nice Spaniards. He recalled the Spaniard who had chatted him up in Earls Court. Would there be dozens, scores, even hundreds lined up for riotous and selfish pleasure, should he fail to achieve the goal of a lasting steady relationship? Had Jet achieved that? The prospects ahead were both exciting and terrifying. How infatuated he'd been with Jet, though they hardly had sex. Jet professed a preference for rough trade. Percy could never be accused of being that. He lay there comatose, wondering what would happen to break the spell. He drifted off into sleep and woke after minutes or hours when Felicity and Margaret appeared with mugs of coffee.

"Oh God, have I got to go and see my parents tomorrow?" Elizabeth said rather candidly. They can throw all my stuff away, if they want. Let's sever the cord, shed the scale," not sure what she was quoting from or how accurately. "Can't I stay here, and you can take me back, Percy."
"But aren't we finished? Isn't it all over between us?"
"I daresay," she said.
"Stay here," said Felicity. "The parents won't notice. Anyway, they're very broadminded."
"But how will we explain it to Albert and Margaret?" asked William.
"Oh, for God's sake," said Percy. "Stay where you like, Elizabeth. I was going to drive you back to Kent, anyway, and it's easier if I don't have to go via Bath. We don't need to alter the sleeping arrangements."
"I shall leave the surgery tomorrow, as planned," Elizabeth stated with slurred certainty, "but will only come as far as here. Then when you drive back you will collect me from here."
"Felicity, shouldn't you ask your parents first?" William said.

148

"Fuck, no," said Felicity. "It's liberty hall here. Another cocktail anyone?"

"Good idea," said Percy, getting into the spirit of things.

"What are the doctor and his wife, my esteemed parents, going to think if they discover their guest, their son's intended, has moved in with some rather louche neighbours, in preference to her distinguished parents?" opined William, being a little obstinate.

"Who are you calling louche, and what does it mean anyway?" Felicity asked, shaking and mixing liquids of different colour and strength, determined to send them all to instant oblivion

"'As if of hemlock I had drunk, and Lethe wards had sunk.' Who wrote that?" asked Elizabeth, feeling it an accurate description of events.

"'My heart aches, and a drowsy numbness pains my sense, as though of hemlock I had drunk, or emptied some dull opiate to the drains one minute past, and Lethe-wards had sunk'," Percy interjected. "It's from *Ode to a Nightingale* by John Keats." He felt rather proud of remembering the full quote. Felicity had finished mixing and passed round her Good Friday cocktails.

"Is this what they drank at the Last Supper?" said Elizabeth in theological mode, "No wonder they all passed out."

"I'm past caring," said Percy, "but is this true love between you and Felicity?"

"I do not doubt my Sapphic persuasions," Felicity said, as if about to give an important press conference. "Today Elizabeth, tomorrow the world."

"I don't like that," said Elizabeth. "You mean you're going to throw me out, before we've even started." She grabbed Felicity and snogged her with all the enthusiasm she could muster. Percy looked on, not knowing what to think, except recalling the lines, "This is the way the world ends, not with a bang, with a whimper."

"Anything to eat?" said William, as if the sight of the frantic snogging had given him an appetite.

"Oh, you've got the munchies, have you?" said Felicity. "Come with me to the kitchen. These two have their lives to sort out." Felicity broke off from her embrace with Elizabeth, rose and grabbed William and took him out of the room.

Percy and Elizabeth sat in embarrassed but soporific silence for a while, till Percy recalled his manners, and ventured to suggest that it wasn't all over and they should try again; but Elizabeth was adamant it had all been a mistake, not that it had been unhappy, but really Percy was that way inclined, and why pretend otherwise? Elizabeth was entirely unsure as to her own real feelings, and this brief encounter with Felicity was the grand sum of any same sex erotic escapades.

"Let's have a cup of tea," said Percy, concluding their heart to heart, and walked with Elizabeth to the kitchen. O horror of horrors! William and Felicity were in flagrante delicto, standing up against the back door. They all sobered up instantly. Elizabeth and Percy left the kitchen, returning to the lounge, whilst William withdrew, feeling ashamed.

"I was enjoying that," said Felicity. "Let's go to my bedroom and resume operations."

"In for a penny, in for a pound, why not?" thought William, dimly aware he had already humiliated his brother, and might further add to an estrangement that could blight their lives. He followed Felicity upstairs.

"I still want a cup of tea," said Percy with all the assertiveness he could muster, and went back into the kitchen, closely followed by Elizabeth, who really didn't know what to do or say.

"I think that Felicity is on drugs," Percy said, "and we should forget everything that's happened."

"Yes, but it's still finished between us, and I've finished with my parents too, and my loathsome brothers. I'll go back on the train tomorrow, pleading some emergency. But I do love you, Percy. You've been really sweet."

"Let's get the tea made," said Percy. He put the kettle on and held her hand. They were still rather drunk, but Percy felt up to driving home after tea. He made the tea, and they sat there drinking it slowly, thinking of all the things they'd never said to each other and never would. But they felt in harmony, and as if they knew each other better than they ever had. They heard the front door go. It was William leaving. Then Felicity came in and burst into tears. However tempting it might have been to comfort her, they both refrained from physical contact.

"Do you want some tea?" Percy asked in his most reassuring voice.

"No, I don't want any fucking tea. Why don't you both just go?"

"We shall," said Elizabeth, being careful not to say "We will."

"May I use the toilet?"

"You can fucking piss in your knickers, for all I care," replied Felicity, picking up a glass and smashing it.

Percy and Elizabeth left the room, and headed straight for the front door, only to bump into Mr and Mrs Sheridan, who were both affable and inebriated, and the dog, which wasn't.

"Thought I just saw you on the road," said Mr Sheridan.

"That would have been my twin. This is Elizabeth. We're late getting back."

Percy grabbed Elizabeth's hand, and moved off. Whilst he didn't want to be rude, this was no time for politeness, particularly as the dog was yapping.

"We must go. Goodbye."

Mrs Sheridan looked slightly flummoxed, but put it all down to embarrassment about the pond back at Christmas, rather than Felicity, whose odd behaviour they failed to notice.

Percy drove home a very long way round, stopping at a public convenience for Elizabeth's benefit, hoping his brother would get home first, despite being on foot.

When they got in, William appeared to be having a heart-to-heart with his mother, as they could hear muffled sounds from the downstairs study. Albert was sitting in the dining room imperturbably doing a crossword.

"Tea or coffee, dad."

"Coffee," he replied decisively.

The three sat down together, and any embarrassment was avoided as Albert held forth on medical politics, without being too bothered as to whether they could follow what he was talking about or indeed cared. It was all very soothing, however.

Elizabeth left early on the Saturday, taking the train all the way to Kent. Percy saw her onto the train, and said fond farewells.

Chapter Twenty-Three

Finale

Percy had a distinct memory from about the age of twelve of looking up the word "homosexual," which he had seen in the *Observer* newspaper. "Being sexually attracted to one's own sex" seemed to sum up his feelings. The sex urge was then new to him, but utterly compelling, replacing all those vague feelings of rudeness, curiosity and excitement he had grown up with.

From the very first he had known that boys and girls were different, and as they grew up, boys were supposed to fall in love with girls and marry them, after which, somewhat mysteriously, children would be born. At the same time there didn't seem to be any good reason why boys shouldn't love other boys, and want to hold their hand and kiss them, and girls likewise. He could recall a teacher at his infants' school telling him off for having his arm round another boy's neck as they were walking along. The other boy had his arm round Percy's neck, and they were engrossed in an important conversation. This wasn't exactly unusual behaviour, so the teacher's interference was almost inexplicable; but there was perhaps a clear hint that either the display of affection, or even the affection itself, were wrong. There was another incident in the school playground when the supervisor, Mrs Potter, the caretaker's wife, told him off for being engaged in fisticuffs with a boy from another class, who fancied himself a tough guy. Neither of them was in any physical danger, so her intervention was extraordinary. Where women were concerned, you couldn't win. The fisticuffs were no doubt the courting ritual for a friendship in which they might put their arms round each other's necks. Mr Potter told him off for doing a handstand, because only girls did that. The worst crime of all was to ride a girl's bicycle.

From a limited exposure to art, literature and history, he glimpsed a world where romance flourished between men, and gods fell in love with beautiful youths, who fell in love with their own reflection. In some code of honour women existed only to be rescued by knights who took extravagant oaths of loyalty to each other, fought side by side on the battlefield and held their dying companions in their arms. Then there was the gunpowder plot supposedly given away because someone told their best friend not to be there. There was Richard the Lion-heart's minstrel, and David's lament, "I weep for thee my brother, Jonathan; thy love to me was wonderful, passing the love of women."

Nevertheless, there was an uncomfortable sense of a less happy, sordid world, where men were arrested for nameless, shameful offences in public toilets. In Percy's imagination the men all wore shabby raincoats, of the kind some schoolmasters wore when umpiring cricket games on chilly days at the start of the season. The glittering bars and clubs that Jet had taken him to were very far removed from plastic or gaberdine macs. He could hear people querying his course of action, "You'll be lonely," but wondered how many married homosexuals weren't at heart desperately lonely, despite acquiring wives and children as trophies of bourgeois respectability.

In any event he needed somewhere to live, where he might entertain. He would still have to save for a flat, though not a house. He could continue to stay at the Townsends, and face the angry silence every morning; but the car would need replacing, and how often could he turn up on Jet's doorstep of a weekend? Jet's advice was to find a boyfriend who was a good mechanic. "Let this be your chat up line: 'how good are you with engines?'" Jet's relationship with Dominic seemed to have deteriorated. Though they were still living together, Dominic had a boyfriend called Steve, who worked in a gym and lifted weights. Jet was not convinced Dominic had at last found true happiness, but didn't seem too bothered by the end of their relationship, having a number of irons in the fire. Percy caught up with the Spaniard he had met before. It was not the precursor to romance, but the first of many liaisons.

The summer term got going with a vengeance, Percy continuing to give lifts to Messrs Townsend and Ridley. He enjoyed his teaching, especially Greek set books, but was always slightly uneasy about Tim Russell who must surely know his secret. Perhaps Tim had his own. How involved he was with Mick Baxter was unknown, but Mr Rowntree was not above making snide comments, which always made Percy uneasy, and sigh for a post where he might feel less exposed. Jet suggested he got a post at Holland Park School, where he might certainly teach Latin, even if they had no use for Greek.

He became more friendly with Roger Duvivier, with whom there seemed to be some sort of tacit understanding, though they made no formal admissions. Percy said he had split with Elizabeth, because they weren't right for each other. Roger asked Percy to go on holiday with him when the term finished. He wanted to visit the North French coast in his Zephyr, which would easily take all the camping equipment, which had been used, when his father was alive, on family holidays. France was always full of adventure. Percy couldn't give a definite answer, but Roger said that the offer was there, because he was going anyway. He was reluctant to part with the Zephyr, though it was very expensive to run, just because of its carrying capacity; but if he were to get something new, he had his eye on a Hillman Husky. Percy suggested they might see a show in London, wondering if he might then take

155

Roger into the Salisbury in St Martin's Lane, a gay venue as well as a pre-theatre bar; but Roger was reluctant. Percy slightly had the impression Roger was under his mother's thumb, and in exchange for allowing him two or three-weeks' summer holiday, she expected his company of an evening.

Percy didn't really have time to think about this, because Jet contacted him to say Dominic had now left, and would Percy consider moving in and sharing the rent and bills. Percy leapt at the chance.

"Your charming friend who sold me the Dover Plan," said Mr Townsend, releasing Percy of any obligation for a month's notice. "The investment reports are good, and I don't think your Morris Minor has long to go, nor does Mr Ridley. Move to London, they say, and you'll never tire of it, not according to Dr Johnson, at any rate. It'll be a long journey, mind, from Earls Court."

It was the journey that finally triggered getting a post at Holland Park to start in September and omitting the nicety of a full term's notice. He confided in Mrs Thompson that the move was dictated by personal reasons, inventing that closeness to Paddington Station would facilitate family visits. He would miss the Greek set books. She said she'd waited her whole career to teach any. Mr Tourtel was sorry to see him leave their tennis club, however limited his involvement had been; but was happy to teach Greek, if required. Mr Rowntree was predictably rather less than pleasant. Percy was throwing away the opportunity to teach Greek to scholarship level in the rarefied atmosphere of one of the country's leading Grammar schools, for a second-rate egalitarian institution, attended by the worst specimens of the lower orders, including coloured people. How could he do that?

"I owe you no explanation," Percy said, but handed over his Greek history teaching notes for the A-level syllabus. They were very neatly handwritten, summarising Bury, with his observations on suitable essay subjects. He had also attempted first drafts of translations of some of the Greek set books, adding as an aside "And these might be useful." Mr Rowntree felt slightly trounced, and abandoned his attempts to intimidate his assistant. They had several applications for the vacancy.

Percy partnered Mrs Tourtel in a club tournament, which they won, sung in the choir concert, and wrote a piece for the school magazine. He said the loves of his life were Greek drama, tennis and singing. He urged every boy to have sport and culture in their lives. If football, rugby or cricket were not for them, there was tennis, badminton, squash, lacrosse, as well as cycling, walking, running, rock climbing etc. He mentioned his interest in wild flowers. He stressed his commitment to education, and thought the best of the grammar school traditions would be preserved in the comprehensive framework, which he believed in. He made no allusions to personal reasons for moving to London, nor attempted even in a guarded way to suggest the ancient world may have had different ideas to the Christian west on important aspects of human instinct. Homosexual practices were illegal after all, and he hardly wished to be seen as a corrupter of youth.

He did go on holiday with Roger Duvivier, who, away from his domineering mother and the repressive English culture, showed some talent for sexual encounters in unlikely places. They enjoyed French cuisine, and got to both Rouen cathedral and William the Conqueror's tomb. He heard from Elizabeth to say she had a new man in her life, and her brief fling with Felicity was only a temporary aberration. Unfortunately, Felicity's aberrations may have been down to drugs, for she died of an overdose, as Percy discovered when he went to Truro

157

later in the summer. He buried the hatchet with his brother for them both to put roses on her grave.

He returned to London for life in the squalid Earls Court flat with Jet, and many a one-night stand in the search for the big lasting romance, sustained all the while by the classical education he had received and which he tried to impart.

THE END